The *Most*
Beautiful
Monday in 1961

The Most Beautiful Monday in 1961

a novel

Ruth F. Brin

Lerner • Minneapolis

Text Copyright © 2008 by Ruth F. Brin

Quotation in Chapter 13 from "The Great Magicians" by C. Day Lewis; published in *The Complete Poems*, Stanford University Press

Lerner Publishing Group
241 First Avenue North
Minneapolis, MN 55401 U.S.A.

Website address: www.lernerbooks.com

Library of Congress Cataloguing-in-Publication Data
Brin, Ruth Firestone.
  The most beautiful Monday in 1961 : a novel / by Ruth F. Brin.
    p. cm.
  ISBN 978-0-9777121-9-9
  1. Jewish women--Fiction. 2. Jews--United States--Fiction. 3. Saint Paul (Minn.)--Fiction. I. Title.
  PS3503.R553M67 2007
  813'.54--dc22
                                        2007037099

Manufactured in the United States of America
1 2 3 4 5 6 BP 13 12 11 10 09 08

For my son, David M. Brin, whose originality, encouragement and editorial skills brought this book to fruition.

✢ CHAPTER 1 ✢

I am a poet without a language, a scientist without systematic knowledge, a woman without a lover. I am a dealer in the mysteries of souls; my motherly compassion can be hired by the hour, and most people regard me as a person set apart. I was an eyewitness to all that happened. But what does an eyewitness know of events, even when she is a psychiatrist? I have probed and searched my evanescent memory, yet I must confess that I know only in part; but what I know, what I witnessed amidst thunder and lightning and the blast of foghorns was a true and transcendent act of love, of heroism, and about such an event no human being has a right to be silent.

Already it is hard to recapture the mood of the beginning of that July day a few weeks ago. It was sunny and warm and we were off on a holiday, playing hooky, the men called it. I remember I opened the door of my apartment in St. Paul to Emory Falk. He stood in the hall, a well-built, fair-haired man wearing white shorts, white t-shirt, and thick-soled canvas shoes. He was impatient to be off, but he said to me, "You're looking well, Charlotte," and looked at me directly enough to make me feel he meant it. I was wearing a full cotton skirt, a bright print, and a white shirt, rather unprofessional, but then, this was a holiday. I'm dark and short and a little stout, and I know a full skirt isn't flattering, but I wanted to be comfortable. Besides, I said to myself, I'm the mother of a young man in graduate school and I don't need to look as thin as a railroad tie. I thought how kind it was of Emory to be gallant as he ushered me down the stairs and held open the heavy door leading to the street. He made me feel feminine, and he seemed young and trim, but when he stepped into the sunshine I noticed how weathered his face looked, with squint marks around his blue eyes when he glanced up at the sky.

"Great day for boating!" he said, "Monday's my favorite day to be on the river, and the weather looks fine. Most beautiful Monday in 1961!" I wondered if he was being too hearty and cheerful.

"Hi!" Ginny, his wife, greeted me from the front seat of their station wagon as Emory opened the back door for me. At first glance, she always looks too young to be Emory's wife. Her hair is shiny red (perhaps she helps it stay that way). She was wearing pink linen shorts and a pink shirt, a combination that emphasized her pink and white skin and her lazy sensuousness. Shorts, yes, to show off the well-proportioned legs, but pink? She wasn't really dressed for athletics. There was just enough mascara on her pale lashes to make them black against her cheek.

"Did I tell you Sol's coming?" she asked, "And Frank and Aggie Segal, you know them, don't you? And we're going to picnic and swim and water-ski and maybe go fishing and be gone all day long!" She motioned to the back part of the station wagon and I saw it was loaded with a picnic basket, towels, swim suits, fishing tackle, and numerous boxes and bags. Ginny explained that although there were chairs, silverware and plates on the boat, you always had to bring more. Emory put my little bag in with the rest and turned onto Summit Avenue, St. Paul's grand boulevard of old mansions and towering elm trees.

We stopped at Sol's house, which was on a nearby street. He was the rabbi of the Reform Temple that I belonged to; he occasionally referred a patient to me. And I knew that he had lost his young wife a few months before. After a difficult struggle, she died of cancer. Their children were quite young; Daniel was ten and Debbie only seven.

As Emory walked up to the red brick house, Ginny commented that they had to urge Sol to take a day off with them. He had hardly had a break since his wife died and Emory thought he would enjoy the day on the river. Her tone seemed to indicate they were performing an act of charity. It crossed my mind that perhaps she would speak of me in the same tone of voice to someone else, poor Charlotte, the refugee, now her boy's gone to Columbia and she's really alone. I discovered later that she had invited me to be an ally in a social situation that she dreaded. At that time the only sign I had that she was nervous was that she was chattering so much. She seemed worried about inviting the Rabbi on a kind of holiday trip. But he was past the period of deep mourning and I had recently met Sol at two other social occasions. I didn't notice any deference in his congregants' behavior toward him. It was not like Europe, where the Rabbi was always treated as an important authority. Yet in spite of outward appearances, I thought, there is always a certain constraint toward Sol, just as there is toward me, toward any professional observer of human behavior, a kind of carefulness to appear natural, not to treat us differently from anyone else, like certain liberals with Blacks or Jews, the comparison amused me. Yes, rabbis and psychiatrists make up a special minority in the human race, set apart.

Sol Gordon is taller than Falk, lanky; what's left of his hair is dark. Loping down the walk with Emory he looked almost gloomy, and certainly older than his friend, though he isn't, they're both in their middle forties. He sat down next to me and I looked into his marvelously scarred face. From the corner of his left eye the scarred area runs down his cheek almost to the corner of his mouth. I was told this happened to him during the war. This rabbi carries his scar where all may see, I thought. I am a woman of scars, and I know this about scar tissue: it is stronger and less elastic than normal tissue. People come to me and I reassure them: your wound will heal, you may be marked but you will be stronger than before, and sometimes they are; and sometimes they die of the wound. Most of my scars—the German scar, the Nazi scar, the human scar—most of them deepen where I carry them, unseen, and they ache when I look at a man like Sol Gordon, a man who carries evidence of war on his own face.

"Well, Charlotte," Sol said to me, pronouncing the final "e" as he knew it was pronounced in German, "How are you?"

"Very well," I said, "and I hope you are too."

He shrugged his shoulders, but he was smiling. Ginny chattered on, about half a tone higher than her usual voice, explaining that the Segals were coming in their own car and would meet us at the marina. Words of condolence were in order, but I could hardly offer them while Ginny dominated the conversation. We drove back to Summit and then to the highway. I thought of the days when my son Bill, then eleven years old, and I had come to St. Paul. A volunteer had driven us around the Twin Cities to see our new home. I was surprised at how blatant the advertising was in downtown St. Paul. I could read the signs, but wondered how my accent would sound, because my first English teacher had been British. The volunteer showed us the Jewish neighborhood and the sprawling University of Minnesota. Bill noticed that everybody lived in houses instead of apartment buildings.

Emory drove rapidly and skillfully, commenting joyously on the new highways that got you out of town so fast; he drove with a kind of nonchalance and ease and he clearly took pride in the new roads and the new houses mushrooming in what had been farmers' fields a year or two before.

It was almost as though he owned the land he sped through, and I understood his feeling of freedom as he waved his arm out the open window and commented on the fine day. It was his car, new and running well, his boat, his day to do with as he pleased, and we were his guests, his friends, there to accept the pleasures he gave us, and to feel no indebtedness toward returning them. He had an openness of spirit to which Sol responded with his crooked smile (the scar forever pinned one side of his mouth from really smiling) and Sol and I looked at each other like parents of a young boy, enjoying his enjoyment of some new plaything.

We drove past a small lake, part of it bridged by the highway, a few summer cottages lining its far side. I am always surprised at how many lakes dot the flat landscape of Minnesota. The original mountains, I was told, had been leveled by a glacier that left the lakes and the big valleys of the rivers as the melting water ran down. The timber had been lumbered in the nineteenth century and only now were large trees returning to the landscape. In the early nineteenth century, St. Paul grew rapidly as the northern-most place on the Mississippi that could be navigated by steam ships.

"Tanner's Lake," Emory said, "Do you know when my grandfather came here just after the Civil War there was a Sioux village here? They traded at grandpa's store, feathers and blankets and all. That was when the store was on First Street, half a block from the boat landing, level with the river. Later we moved the store uptown."

"Indians," I said, "we used to read those Wild West books by Karl May when we were kids in Germany, perhaps you didn't know that, I half hoped for Indians when I came here."

"The sequel is," Emory said, "that chief's grandson was at Harvard when I was there. He's a minister now, with an interracial church in Harlem."

"That's some kind of an irony, isn't it?" Ginny said. She sat with her arm along the back of the front seat, half turned toward us, so that we saw her in profile. For her day outdoors she wore a gold wristwatch set with rubies and diamonds. Her arm lay along the back seat, white, curved, sensuous, the hands soft, the fingers curved idly, gracefully.

"I'm afraid I'm going to burn today," she said. "Charlotte, you're so lucky to be dark. I despise my pale skin, it's so useless."

"Now dear," Emory said.

"Emory likes it," she said, "he was glad when the girls were born with fair complexions." She patted her fluffy, shiny waves. I wondered if Sol thought that a bare arm, with an expensive wristwatch, was provocative, sexy, and when I glanced at his face as his dark eyes widened just a little, I thought that he did.

As we drove the land began to tilt a little, and then we came to the new steel and concrete bridge that had been completed that spring. The Mississippi River lay below us, its majestic hills dwarfed by our height. But as soon as we had crossed the bridge, turned off the highway, and taken the steep dirt road that winds down to the marina, the hills began to grow and stretch and assume the proportions of mountains.

"This town was just about dead for years," Emory said. "Of course it was a great lumber town 100 years ago, but this boating craze has really picked things up. There's a lot of business here now."

We stopped at a parking lot where an attendant waved Emory toward a parking place and then ambled up to take some instructions about filling extra gas tanks to put on board.

There was a floating dock and a berth for each boat, of which there were many kinds. Sol walked beside me and I asked him if he knew much about boats.

He grinned, "This summer I'm getting to be the floating rabbi," he said. "I've been on Harris' speedboat, and Morton's sailboat with cabin and auxiliary motor, and Goldberg's cabin cruiser that he bought from the Crosby's, and I've even been out in a Park Board canoe with my own kid. He says ya gotta have a boat these days, and that seems to be the idea."

We walked to the end of the floating dock and looked out at the Mississippi River, lying sparkling in the sunshine below wooded hills, some conical as picture book mountains, some topped with farmhouses or red barns with tall silos, but all cut with deep ravines where the evergreens showed up dark and thick against the paler green of the deciduous trees. To me it was a great relief from the flat prairie landscape, more like Europe.

Emory came along behind us, his arms loaded with boxes and bags from the back of the station wagon.

"You know what I kept thinking last September when we were in Europe?" he said. "First we thought we wouldn't go to Germany. But then we did, we went down the Rhine, just the way I did with my family when I was a kid, all I could think of was my river at home. Right here. The Rhine is supposed to be so beautiful and all, but look at this!"

He was right, of course, merely one crumbling castle and perhaps a terraced vineyard would have brought the Rhine to this very spot, but I felt the muscles around my mouth tightening when he spoke of it, and I only nodded agreement. It was as though he had taken the charming landscape I looked at, sparkling in the morning sun, and had painted a spiked helmet over the hills and strong barbed wire between the water and me. Now he turned to show us his boat, floating at its berth with a canvas rooftop sheltering it. He told us it was a 30-foot cabin cruiser. I saw a deck with comfortable red and blue canvas chairs, an entrance into a cabin, much polished brass and varnished wood. There was a little ladder so you could climb up to the roof of the cabin if you wished, and the instrument panel, much like the dashboard of a car, and steering wheel and captain's tall chair to one side of the deck. I noticed that the captain must look over the cabin to see where he is going.

"Sunday's no good on the river anymore," Emory said as he took a big step onto the boat and set down his load, "but Monday! I love blue water on blue Monday; you have the whole river to yourself. Wait till we get to the sandbar! We'll have the whole thing to ourselves! Gorgeous spot too."

Ginny came down the dock then with the Segals, and Emory greeted them cordially. Frank Segal, heavy-set, jocular, smoking a cigar, had gray curly hair and a pleasant smile. He shook hands with me, and I felt my hand almost lost in his big warm palm. He looked at me in a friendly way and said, "All set?" then turned to Emory, "Say, nice little scow you got here," and kicked at the cruiser with his foot. "Think you got room for all six of us? I'm pretty big, you know."

Emory took him seriously at first, "We've had as many as ten on here, Frank." Then he caught on. "Well, if you're too big we'll put a life jacket on you and tow you out behind!"

Aggie Segal stood alone, a little behind her husband. She too wore shorts, cream-colored, and she had assumed, perhaps unconsciously, a pose that suited her well, the pose of the big-eyed, angular Parisian model, so thin that when you look at her sophisticated stance you remember that she was once a waif of Paris, a hungry child in a blue starched pinafore. The women admire Aggie's long thin body and haunted eyes, but the men watch Ginny with her almost Rubens lushness and her half-smile.

"Where do you want this mix, Ginny?" Emory balanced a wooden case of ginger ale on his knee.

"In the galley, under the bench," she said and he leaped onto the boat and disappeared into the cabin. Then he stuck his head out, "Come on, everybody, what are you waiting for?"

Sol started back toward the car. "I'll help you unload."

"Okay," Emory said, "men unload, women come aboard and relax."

Frank had gone back to get the Segals' bathing suits, and Ginny and Aggie were giggling about what Ginny called "the head." There was a galley in the cabin, and a small space with two built-in benches that could be beds, a folding dining table, and several places to "stow gear" as Emory said. He was loading extra gasoline, water-skis and fishing tackle and I put my little bag with my bathing suit on the bench.

Frank Segal's good-natured voice boomed out, "What would the poor people think?" as Emory brought in a paper bag with the tops of liquor bottles sticking out, "and on Monday too. Oi!"

Certainly the expedition had a carefree beginning, and none of us imagined how it would end.

⚜ CHAPTER 2 ⚜

"*E*verything aboard, Ginny? Shall I cast off?" Emory called.

"Okay," she answered. She had a rather high voice and her red hair was sparkling in the sun.

Frank guffawed, "You got to say, 'aye, aye, sir' matey" he said. She looked at him almost as though he'd insulted her, then turned to enter the cabin; as she passed me I saw her eyes had deepened, with a kind of wounded deer look. I wondered if she was really as defenseless as she looked. Frank was sprawled in a deck chair, his broad shoulders almost bigger than the back of the chair, his abdomen like a ball—I had heard Americans say, "a potbelly like a watermelon." He wasn't thinking about overweight, I thought, but about having a good time. Emory finished with the ropes, jumped on board, and began to fiddle with the dashboard.

The motor started with a jerk and a roar; then he backed the boat skillfully out into the river. The vibration was shocking to me, the throbbing of the motor seemed to shake my whole body, and the floorboard moved like a live thing. How could we carry on any conversation above all that noise? My friends didn't seem to notice. Frank stood by the railing at the rear of the boat, his legs spread a little apart, but looking comfortable. Ginny was in the cabin, Aggie sat in a deck chair behind Emory, and Sol sprawled in a canvas deck chair, his long legs extended, his bony hand supporting his scarred cheek. I sat beside him. Of course they all knew what to expect, and all Americans have a remarkable tolerance for noise. Some of my patients are most uneasy when it's quiet.

Frank pulled a cigar out of his shirt pocket and tried to light it.

He strolled over toward Emory, "Say, you boat owners opposed to smoking? How're you supposed to light these goddamn things in this wind?"

Emory looked up and grinned, then he took a lighter from a pocket below the dashboard, "Here, try this."

Frank succeeded in puffing his cigar almost immediately. He nodded his head at Emory, chose a deck chair near Aggie and sat himself down with a great "Ahhh!" Then he grinned, "Not bad for a poor north side boy!" he said taking the cigar out of his mouth to speak, and then replacing it. I knew the north side of Minneapolis was where most Jews still lived, although young couples were moving to a suburb called St. Louis Park. Frank was the sort of man who took a certain pleasure in making fun of himself, not too much; perhaps it's not so bad a way to be, I thought.

Sol looked up at the hills, and I looked too. It still seemed too noisy to try to raise my voice to speak, and I turned my face toward the forested hills.

As we moved along I noticed the sun shining on the opposite bank of the river, picking out a white farmhouse that turned to dazzling, shimmering light, while we moved in sudden cool shade, as a great cloud came over us, a gray piled up cumulus, threatening. It was the first warning of the day. The river turned gray and opaque, and a wind made it choppy, like a great hand run the wrong way along its back, making the waves rise in fear, but across the river all was still and bright, like my childhood. My mother, *meine Mutti*, I see her face as she leans over me to say goodnight, incredibly young, her long hair down to her shoulders, she is in her nightgown, and her brown eyes are pools of love, she calls me *"liebchen,"* and I see my father in his business suit, with the watch chain across his vest, and he calls me *"das Kind* (the child)" and I am afraid, because what he keeps saying is "don't tell the child," but I am a young girl, twelve or thirteen, conscious that my breasts are budding, and I do not want to be a neutral child, he is robbing me of my coming womanhood, my blooming, and he will not tell me, but I want to know! He wanted to keep Fascism from me, anti-Semitism from me, as if he could, poor, puzzled man. My nurse walked me to school, and brushed my hair for me, and starched my aprons, and taught me how to embroider and make lace. When she walked with me, they didn't call names. The dark clouds gathered over my head, over my childhood, and they didn't tell me, I had my eyes on something bright and distant, and now it all lies across a river I cannot cross again, a dark, a bloody, horrible river. They were dumped in the camps, like loads of sand, my people, my father, my dear, lovely mother. I will not think of the camps. I will remember my parents as they were: good, serious people, thoughtful. Father, after a glass of wine in the evening, taking out his violin, and playing. Oh he played like an angel, I thought, my heart rose with his cadenzas, and his bow seemed to stroke me, and mother accompanying him, I remember seeing her black shoe on the piano pedal, with shoe buttons, the kind you button with a hook, how long ago that was! How long ago, across how many rivers and oceans of time.

Those clouds, the first warning, seemed to melt away behind the hills. I made an effort to listen to the conversation around me. Frank and Emory were talking about someone's contribution to the Fund, someone whose card Frank had. That means Frank was supposed to get his pledge.

I knew the Fund was like a Jewish Community Chest (both unlike anything in Europe). Jews raised money and gave it to local, national, Israeli, and international Jewish charities. It was one of these groups, Hebrew Immigrant Aid Society, that had sent someone to meet Bill and me at the docks in New York, and had arranged for us to come to Minnesota. Their policy, they explained, was to send refugees around the U.S. where the local Jewish community would be helpful, although if we were unhappy we could move again. People helped us there too.

Emory said "I don't think George has got much."

"Whaddya mean?" Frank challenged. "He made a killing on that hoola hoop deal. The toy business is crazy, a new corporation for every new toy!"

These two men never seem to agree on anything, I thought and wondered what was the underlying source of the tension.

Now they were talking about someone they called Irv. Emory thought he should pledge more but Frank questioned whether he could afford it. "He was a tubby kid," he commented, "went to Talmud Torah with me and flunked out when he was eleven. He didn't finish the U either. (When people from this area talk about "the U" it means the University of Minnesota.) I don't think he's smart enough to make a lot of money."

Then they mentioned a third man, Jim.

Emory appealed to Sol. "What do you think Jim would be able to give? They just built a new house."

Sol responded, "People don't show me their bank balances, or their moral balances either. But it surprises me sometimes how everybody seems to know everybody else's income."

Aggie remarked, "The Jewish community here is just like a small town. We all know each other's business."

Ginny interrupted, "I hear Jim and Esther went to Europe and came back with a Matisse, and in their new house there's a small room with practically nothing in it except the painting. I'd like to see that, even if French impressionists are somewhat passé. I'd prefer a Jackson Pollack myself."

"You'll be invited there at the end of the campaign. They have agreed to give a dinner for the big givers," Emory told her. "I'm glad the hospital is up and running now. That was certainly a big money raising effort. Until the campaign, I didn't even know that Jewish doctors weren't on the staffs of any hospitals in Minneapolis."

"No kidding," Frank grimaced, "the goyish doctors got a rakeoff whenever Jewish doctors had to ask them to admit their patients. I'm glad that charming kind of discrimination is finished. What will they come up with next?"

"Well, sometimes I think you are oversensitive," Emory muttered.

I looked up at the sky, clear again, except for one

low cloud in the east. We had come to a place where the valley was wider, the hills set further back from the river itself, a place, I knew, which had once been filled by a great glacier. When I write poetry, I write in my native language, in German, poetry for a dead generation, dead on one side of the barbed wire, or dead on the other. Words began to float through my mind.

"I don't know how they say this in English, 'I lift my eyes to the mountains?' It doesn't sound right."

"Rabbi," I asked, "How does that psalm go, 'I raise my eyes to the hills?'"

"It's usually translated, 'I will lift up mine eyes to the mountains,'" he said, "'from whence cometh my help.'"

I started to laugh. "What is that 'up' doing in there? When I write English I'm already putting in too many 'alreadys' and 'ups.' My English teacher would have made me write, 'I will raise my eyes,' period. 'No Germanisms, please,' he would say, 'lift already *schon noch* implies the 'up.' So maybe there's an 'up' in the Hebrew?" I asked.

"You know you're right," Sol said, "I never thought of it; no, there's only one verb in the Hebrew, there seldom are any prepositions in Hebrew anyway, 'I will raise my eyes to the mountains,' I like that, of course this verb also means, oh, to look hopefully toward something, not just 'raise,' but you can't put it all in."

"From whence my help cometh," I added. "Why

was help supposed to come from the mountains?"

Emory had been listening to us. "I suppose it's a primitive idea, isn't it, Rabbi? That God lived in the mountains. That must be a very ancient psalm, but it doesn't bother me that it's primitive."

"It needn't bother you," Sol said dryly, "it certainly is ancient and pre-dates the Babylonian exile, but the psalmist did not believe that God lived in the mountains. This is a song of *aliya*, of ascending, of going up, of making the pilgrimage to Jerusalem. Jerusalem was on top of the mountain, and in Jerusalem was the Temple where the spirit of God sometimes dwelled. Not always." He repeated the next line in Hebrew and then translated "'My help is from the Lord, who makes heaven and earth,' not from a spirit living in a mountain. I think some translations might say 'made.' Tense in Hebrew is another story, but I prefer the present, a process going on all the time, 'the Lord who makes heaven and earth.'" Yes, Judaism was complex from the beginning; monotheism was certainly not a primitive concept and it dominates Jewish thinking.

Ginny climbed out of the galley then with a tray of drinks in her hands and walked toward Aggie. The boat moved forward evenly, noisily, but as she got there she lurched forward, and one glass toppled forward and spilled on Aggie's lap. "Oh, I'm so sorry!" Ginny shrieked, backing away, "I didn't mean…" Aggie was on her feet and Emory brought a towel. He began to wipe at her shorts and she took the towel from him. I wondered why Ginny was so hostile to Aggie. "I didn't mean to," she said, making me realize that of course she did mean to.

Frank was piloting the boat now. "Hey, boss, how do you put this thing in reverse?" Emory motioned to the gear shift, there was a sickening feeling through my body as the boat lurched, began to move slowly backwards, all the whirlpools on the side trying to move in the opposite direction suddenly, like the little whirlpools in my stomach. Yet no one else seemed to mind. Now Frank jerked us forward again, back to our course; even Ginny balanced her tray without spilling. No one seemed to feel as I did, the inevitability of the six of us being pulled on this journey together, in this little wooden shell; no one seemed to mind the constant noise of the motor, the vibrations, the movement, which never let go of us for a moment. We were not going toward the hills, only between them, we were not climbing toward the Lord who makes heaven and earth, but being propelled toward some common and as yet unknown fate.

Ginny had served everyone, and when she brought me my glass, she leaned over and almost whispered, "Come in the galley with me. I've got to talk to you."

❧ CHAPTER 3 ❧

*G*inny sat across from me on the bunk. Her shoulders were rounded and her eyes seemed large and dark, with the peculiar quality of the red-haired person's eyes, deepening from green-blue into almost black as she looked up at me, her face partly in shadow. She did not look with hope, as Sol had said, but with tension; her lower lip trembled and she gripped the side of the bunk tightly, so her knuckles looked almost white. I sat back a little, inwardly sighing, assuming the professional calm I thought she was looking for.

"This is a terribly difficult day for me," she began, "I hope you don't mind my asking you in here, I really need your help," she bit her lip and then released it. "I have my reasons for wanting to avoid Frank, if possible for the whole day. I don't want to get into conversation with him. Please don't leave me alone with him and interrupt if he starts talking to me. Will you do that?"

"I can try, but I don't understand."

"No. Well, I've always avoided them, socially, at the club. When they joined the Temple, I was upset, but it's big enough so I can avoid them. Then when she came into the hospital auxiliary I had to quietly quit working there, and I'd been very devoted to that work. But I had known Frank…once…and I didn't want Emory to know about it.

"Emory and Frank are in a business deal together, something about a new shopping center, you know, this isn't just a day off for them; it's a chance to talk business. I told Emory to invite Frank to play golf, they could talk at the club, I didn't want to have to spend a whole day with Frank! But Emory says Frank is a better golfer than he is and that gives Frank the psychological advantage, and Emory wants to be in the driver's seat. It's our boat. You just have to help me avoid Frank and Aggie!"

"But my dear," I said, "after all, we are six people on a small boat, how can I do that?"

I waited while she brushed back her hair with her hand, her left hand with the jeweled wristwatch. "It isn't easy to avoid people in this town, people who think they belong, I never thought Frank would be one of those people. I told Emory he shouldn't have any business deal with him unless he belonged, but Emory wouldn't listen to me about Frank. He said they had already struck a deal. I tried to talk him out of it, but he didn't understand and wouldn't listen."

I can always tell when someone feels compelled to confide in me. Of course, I would prefer to listen only to my patients, because these outside confidences are far too superficial. I can't imagine what Freud would have said if he had Ginny on his couch, but he would have looked for sexual problems and I suspected a sexual tension between Ginny and Frank.

Emory poked his head in the door of the galley, "Come on out, girls, the sun is shining!" He said it cordially, but he moved his head in a way that seemed to signal to Ginny she had to move. Frank stood in the doorway behind him. Ginny and I got up and the two men brushed past us in the narrow passageway. I noticed that Ginny shrank back so Frank wouldn't touch her.

Emory said, "Watch Sol and see that he doesn't get into any trouble, he's piloting for us." Ginny nodded and we went back on deck. I could hear the men's voices in the cabin, but not distinctly enough to hear their words. Aggie was sitting close to Sol watching him drive the boat. With the Rabbi in control, it still vibrated with the same noisy rumble, but I thought I was beginning to get used to it. The noise was what made it hard to overhear the men in the cabin. They had a certain privacy that way, and apparently Ginny thought we did, too. She leaned toward me as I sat there and half whispered, "I've got to tell you about it," she said. "I came out here, west, one summer to visit my aunt. It was after my sophomore year in college."

Neither of us had seen Aggie drift toward us, but now she stood quite close, and interrupted, "You went to Wellesley, didn't you?"

Ginny jumped. Then she looked down at her lap, "No, Vassar," she stopped. She couldn't go on and she hadn't the presence of mind to change the subject. "We were talking about colleges," I said, "and where to send one's young."

"Isn't your son at Columbia?" Aggie asked me, "How does he like it?"

"Very well. How about your Robert?" I really miss Bill: his youth, his cheerfulness, his affection. Yet I know I have to let him go to be his independent self and appreciate every letter I ever get.

"Robert's at Harvard, and his mother barely graduated high school. That's pretty good, isn't it?"

"You didn't go to college?" Ginny asked.

Aggie shook her head. "I tried taking some courses at the University, especially after Robert got interested in art. He didn't know it, I signed up for a history of art course. I guess I got something out of it, but I was too old." She looked at Ginny rather significantly. "I always envy people with college educations."

Rather faintly Ginny said, "I didn't finish, I never got a degree or anything. What did you do, then, did you work?"

"I worked. I worked to support my parents, and I worked to help out my aunt and uncle, and after we were married, I worked for a union, and when Frank went in the service, I worked for the government till I got pregnant. You never worked?"

Ginny shook her head.

"I wonder if you know what the depression was like for people like me and my family," Aggie said. "I couldn't help thinking about it this morning, taking a weekday off was unheard of! I wonder if you could imagine, while you were there at Vassar with all those rich girls."

Ginny said, "They weren't all rich, many were on scholarship—the bright ones."

Aggie didn't hear or couldn't. She continued. "I wonder if you know what it was like to work for fifteen dollars and fifty cents a week. I remember my paycheck, it was yellow, and I remember the hopelessness, my mother sick and old, and my aunt and uncle, all of us crowded together in that old gray duplex that was never painted. Nobody had any money for paint in those days."

Frank and Emory emerged from the galley door. "Whatcha talking about, Ag?" Frank asked.

"The thirties, the depression, the misery, the hopelessness."

"Miserable, yes," said Frank, "but not hopeless. I always think there was a real stirring in those days. Roosevelt was a leader, a man you could believe in, and the whole social complexion of this country changed. Floyd Olson, the governor, was great too. I'll never forget the truck strike, the excitement, the feeling of purpose, of the masses moving forward. Were you in Minneapolis then, Emory?"

"Not exactly," Emory said. "We weren't perhaps so concerned with the strike. My father, of course, deplored the whole thing, thought that a closed shop would be a limitation on the individual worker's rights. He thought he was being a good liberal by standing up for the individual rights of workers rather than have a union order them around."

"Damn right," Frank retorted, "liberal, who-owned-a-big-store-himself point of view. It's easier to keep 'em down that way. What were you doing that summer anyway, helping out the Citizens' Alliance? Your old man must have been a loyal member of that employers' outfit."

Emory stiffened. "Virginia and I were on our honeymoon in Europe. I was never personally involved. Of course I knew that the Trotskyites had moved into the city. You were supporting them, weren't you?"

"Nope, but I was on their side. Even spent a night in jail with one of them, wonderful guy, too, didn't I, Ag?" He looked at her with a reminiscent fondness.

"Yeah, you were a fighter in those days, Frank," she responded.

"Because of you."

Ginny said a little weakly, "I guess our '30s were a lot different from yours. And yours, too, Charlotte."

"Mine? All I can say is, it was a lot worse in

Germany: depression we had, and strikes, and unemployment, and a large dose of that hopelessness Aggie spoke of. There were legless and armless men on the streets, wounded in the First World War, begging. There was the madness of a huge inflation. And there was the terrible growing anti-Semitism. Studying at the Jewish hospital helped keep my mind busy, but I couldn't leave till 1939. After *Kristallnacht* the hospital was also destroyed." Germany was a boat on a stormy river, and we were the Jonahs they threw overboard to drown, but I stopped talking about it. These innocent Americans weren't interested in my history, only in their own.

"We've lost something," Frank was saying, "a sense of purpose, a sense of decency. The labor movement has lost something vital; we thought we were building a labor party that would be a people's party, like in Great Britain, that would move toward real social justice. Hell! Now the labor movement's full of gangsters and the average workman's more worried about making payments on his second car than he is about any other damn thing. No solidarity. No sense of values any more."

"You make too many speeches," mumbled Aggie.

"It's my opinion," Emory said, "that the average workman never did care about anything but his bread and butter. Leadership comes from the intelligent and the educated; sure, during the period of immigration labor had good leaders, men who were intelligent and shrewd, if denied education in

Europe for one reason or another. I'm not surprised at the state of labor leadership, in this country anybody with brains gets himself an education, leaves the working classes, and makes money."

Aggie nodded her head, "That's what happens. Guys like Frank make money and speeches."

"Now honey," Frank said, "you know."

"Yes, I know," her voice grated a little, "I was only saying, maybe it would have looked different if guys like you had stayed in the movement. Not you personally." Frank looked slightly wounded.

"But look honey," she said, "you're not the only one. They've all pulled out."

"Excuse me," said Ginny, over-brightly, "I'm getting too hot out here and I'm afraid I'm going to get sunburned. Charlotte, you look warm, too, would you like to come inside with me for a while?"

"Certainly," I said, thinking her a little obvious but knowing she was bound to go on with our conversation. We squeezed into the cabin and sat on the two benches that had storage underneath. I realized I would have to listen again as I saw her straighten her shoulders and look at me—and then suddenly lower her eyes. Pink shorts and shirt didn't seem quite the costume for a confession, but for her it was.

Ginny seemed better controlled now. "I'm going to begin at the beginning," she said. "I'm going to tell you the whole story. I never really have before, told anyone, I mean." As I remember it now, I think she talked almost an hour, while we kept chugging, moving, pounding on down the river. This is how her story went:

Ginny had wanted to go to Europe that summer, but her father said that keeping her at Vassar was expensive enough and he simply couldn't afford it. As she rode in the coach from New York, she kept thinking of Renée. Renée would be in France this summer and she, Ginny, would be stuck visiting her dear Aunt Lydia in Minneapolis. What would she have to tell the girls she'd gone to prep school with, or the others in Lathrop Hall when she got back to school? Renée had friends in France, including a young count she'd met skiing in Switzerland two years before. Betty, another college friend, was going home to Kansas, of course, but her father never interfered with her evenings and she had a young man named Tom she'd been going with since high school. She told amusing stories about Tom forgetting his "safeties," and Tom hiding behind the sofa when her father came home. Betty was bright and attractive, she'd wiggle her hips and say, "After all, what else is there to do in a small town in the evening?" Ginny never admitted to Renée or Betty how little experience she'd had, they both seemed to know so many men. Why had her mother insisted on her going to a girls' prep school? How did you ever meet men? Of course, Mother wanted her to get into Vassar and she couldn't have done it without private schooling. She often went home to New York on weekends, pretending to have some big date, but aimlessly going shopping or to some museum with her mother instead.

Aunt Lydia had told her to take a cab from the Minneapolis railroad station, because the judge would have the car downtown until 6 p.m., and she didn't drive anyway. This was typical of Aunt Lydia, who never did anything herself, not even answering the telephone. She trained her maids to take a message and she would call back if she thought it important. Ginny came out of the railroad station to the hot street. She blinked in the sunshine. The porter put her bags in the cab and she gave the Lake Harriet Boulevard address to the driver.

He turned around and smiled at her, "Isn't that Judge Kaufman's house?" By the time they had reached the big Spanish style house, he knew she was the judge's niece, visiting for the summer, and she knew he was Frank Segal, working his way through the University driving a cab. She was attracted by his size, his smile, and the fact that he was driving a cab to get through school. When she asked him what he was studying, he said, "philosophy," but when she asked him something about which courses, he said, "It doesn't matter." Later she learned he was really in law school. His mother said he should be a lawyer, he might as well get paid for talking so much. Ginny laughed when he quoted his mother.

"Really, what kind of an accent is that?" He told her Polish, or Yiddish, or both.

"Really," he mimicked her. It would be fun to tell

the girls about a student cab driver with a mother with a foreign accent, she thought. What about Aunt Lydia? How closely would she supervise her social life this summer? Ginny wondered how she'd get Frank to call her, but that wasn't so hard; he asked, just before he drove up to her aunt's house, if he might call her some time, and she said yes.

Aunt Lydia kissed her formally; she was always a little formal and remote. She took Ginny upstairs to her room, suggesting that she might want to rest after her journey. Ginny went in the white tiled bathroom and looked at herself in the mirror. Her skin was almost perfect, and her red hair, curly, brushed her shoulders. She thought that Frank must be at least twenty-five, he seemed like a man, not a boy, and she liked that, and she began to think she would have something interesting to tell Renée and Betty when she saw them in the fall.

Suddenly the motor sputtered and stopped. There was a sickening lurch. Ginny held her breath. In the sudden silence, the boat swung to the right; I was convinced the motor had failed. We would never get to our destination, I was sure, as the boat swung loosely to the left. Emory's head appeared in the hatch. "Gas can," he demanded. Ginny opened the cupboard and handed him a red can.

"He didn't have a full tank when we started," she told me. "This should take us all the way." In a few minutes the cruiser resumed its noisy bumpy trip down the river, but my anxiety remained with me.

While she waited for Frank to call, Ginny settled down at Aunt Lydia's. She had the east bedroom, and she made the bed every morning even though Aunt Lydia had two maids; mother insisted that was the proper way for a young lady to behave. She lay on the beach at Lake Harriet the first day, slathering on suntan lotion so she wouldn't burn, and she listened to the judge pontificate at dinner. Sunday evening Aunt Lydia had invited the Falks and another family for a "little supper." She told Ginny she wanted her to meet Emory, who was going to Harvard business school in the fall, but while Ginny sat next to Emory at the table that night, she kept thinking of Frank, and how his eyelashes were so long they touched his cheek when he crinkled up his eyes and laughed.

Afterwards, the judge asked her how she liked "our Emory."

"Fine," she said somewhat weakly.

"Domineering mother," the judge said. "Any son of hers would seem a little anemic. Give him time."

Ginny didn't tell Aunt Lydia or the judge about Frank. He met her on the beach one afternoon; he had walked all the way from the north side, he told her, and she didn't know whether to believe him or not.

"No, really," he said laughing, "I had to give Ma money for groceries this morning, I've got exactly a dime, I wanted to buy you some popcorn at the wagon, after all!" He then began to peel off his clothes.

"Frank!" Ginny's eyes widened.

He seemed amused that he could shock her; he

kept on peeling and she saw that he wore trunks under his slacks. She looked at his powerful chest and the dark curly hair on it and she felt her breath draw in. Men had just begun to wear trunks then, most of them still wore suits with tops, and he seemed shockingly naked to her. He took her hand and ran with her, splashing, into the water. He swam well, too, better than she, and said he had won a swimming race when he was twelve. Afterwards, as they lay on the sand consuming their popcorn, he explained that he would be able to use the cab at 10 that night, and he would call for her. Ginny never understood how he managed it, but every now and then he would call her in the evening. She liked it best when the phone rang when she was in bed, reading. She felt lucky she had a phone in her bedroom.

"Vir-ginia?" he would drawl out her name, "What are you doing?"

"Nothing," she'd say, and feel her lips smiling, "Why?"

"In bed?"

"No," she'd say, and he'd laugh and say, "Bet you are, too." Then he'd tell her to meet him on the corner. She'd throw on some clothes, then slip down the back staircase and out the kitchen door. Aunt Lydia was busy with her bridge and book clubs during the day, and in the evening she and the judge often went out. She didn't pay much attention to Ginny.

"Why don't you belong in the judge's house?" she asked him once.

"I'm just a little north-side Jew," he said.

"So? The Kaufman's are Jews aren't they?"

"Temple Jews," he said, "not my kind. Besides, I hate rich people, all I can think of is my Uncle Jake and how his partner got rich and he ended up bankrupt. Anybody who's rich has cheated somebody."

"Am I rich?"

"You're different!" he would laugh.

The first time he put his arm around her shoulder after he had parked the taxi, Ginny put her head against his hard and exciting chest. She felt his hand on her right arm, then move toward her breast, then touching, touching. How odd, she thought, it reminds me of when the doctor checked me for lumps, is Frank clinical? Or was the doctor sexy? And then he touched the very tip of her nipple, and even through her clothes, she felt a shock that made her tremble and bury her face in his chest. She wriggled from his hand, but he put his hand right back. "So fresh, so young," he murmured, "they keep the girls nice at Vassar, don't they?"

He didn't sleep with her that time, not for several weeks, really, not until she'd got so she waited every night for a call and cried if it didn't come. Another night she cried because Emory had called to invite her to a concert, and she was afraid she'd miss Frank, but she couldn't very well refuse the invitation. She remembered him standing in the front hall with a straw hat in his hand, and the judge telling him to drive carefully.

Emory was very earnest about music, and he liked chamber music best. The summer concerts were light, he explained to her, but the best the town had to offer. She made some remarks based on Renée's music history course that seemed to impress him quite a bit. He told her how he had been working at his father's store. She knew it was the biggest department store in the city, but he made it sound rather small, and was hoping to learn some things "at school" (she knew he meant Harvard) that might help him in the store. He was clearly following the path that had been set for him by his parents. He was not rushing her, but treating her like an adult, as knowledgeable as he was himself. He didn't try to neck that first night either, though he kissed her goodnight on the front porch by the wrought-iron railing and she was afraid Aunt Lydia could see them out her bedroom window. But perhaps she wasn't looking.

On the 4th of July, Frank took her to see the fireworks at North Common. The place was mobbed with families, babies, men and women, boys and girls. Aunt Lydia and the judge had some political affair to attend and thought Ginny was home.

"Working class people," Frank said. "My folks are here, too," but he never took her to meet them. They sat on the damp grass and watched the Roman candles and rockets shoot into the air. She felt Frank's body behind her, warm, big, protecting, and she was at ease with his presence. She'd seen the opera and gone to the theater, but she'd never seen fireworks in a park, not with a man she thought she loved. They didn't drive home afterwards, but Frank parked in a dark lane he knew, and urged her to come in the back seat of his cab.

"I know," he said, "I'll be gentle."

She didn't speak, she waited, afraid yet curious and wanting, she felt his hands, on her breasts first, now the shock was familiar, yet still a shock, then inside her thighs, she wore no stockings, it was strange how she felt she had been waiting for this for a long time, waiting, she heard Betty's voice saying "safeties" and she stirred a little. "Don't worry, darling," Frank said, "I'll take care of everything," and then his mouth was over her mouth, and she no longer could think of words, only of feelings, feeling.

Afterwards he said, "You're lovely," and she shaking, hurting a little, feeling wet and disarranged, said, "Was it all right for you?"

"Next time it'll be better for you, little one," he said, and he patted her cheek. And the next time it was. Lying on the beach in the afternoon by herself she would think, "but I don't really like it. It's awkward and strange, and sometimes I hurt in the morning, why do I want it? What does Betty like about it?" And other times she would sing to herself, "I know now, now I know," and she would look at her Aunt Lydia and the judge and wonder how they looked when they did it, and if they liked it, and whether Lydia was a virgin when she got married. Probably. Like Mother. They were so strictly brought up. Aunt Lydia arranged for her to take Emory and another young couple to a summer theater production. She told Frank all about it, and he said, "I'll take you out some other night." She thought he'd be jealous, but he simply didn't expect her to save every night for him. He called her "little one" or "darling" but he never said, "I love you." She almost said it to him, but she didn't. What am I to him she wondered, just an odd specimen of the upper classes, just a virgin he deflowered, how many has he? She tried to ask him but he put her off with laughter. "You don't want to know everything, do you? That would spoil it."

He didn't speak of love. How could he? After love comes marriage, and he was driving a cab, going to school, and helping support his family. She thought of them as old and bent-over and helpless. He didn't speak of love, and she began to listen to Emory, who called for her at the front door and one evening came with a corsage and took her dancing at the Jewish country club.

He told her how glad he was that she was at school in the east, he didn't know any girls there, would she come to Harvard for a weekend some time? There'd be a football game and a dance. He told her she was lovely looking and the fellows would be jealous of him, he told her after she had dinner at his home that his mother thought she was a lovely girl, too. Isn't this the way it's supposed to be? She told herself, he has family, money, everything, and then she lay in bed waiting for Frank to call, waiting, waiting, she thought of how noble it would be to wait for Frank, to marry him, to work so he could finish school, or go through law school. She didn't know what she meant to him, did he love her? Or was he only trifling? Trifling, that was her mother's phrase. Oh, Mother would have a fit, she thought, an absolute fit. August wore on, hot and still, and Emory came sometimes to the front door, and she ran down the backstairs other times to Frank. She wanted to be important to him, wanted Frank to love her.

It was September then and her last night with Frank. "Don't you know what you mean to me?" she said softly as she lay against him.

"You'll remember me for a little while," he had said, "and, little one, I won't forget, and I won't say goodbye."

"But, Frank."

To his surprise he saw the hurt look in her face, but he said, "Some day you'll marry some rich guy, that's what you've been raised for. Now you know, Gin, I have to help my parents financially and if I'm going to get myself through school I have to keep my nose to the grindstone. I thought you and I were just having a little summer play."

"Don't say that! I'll wait for you."

"I'm sorry you took it so seriously, but you mustn't wait for me. Forget all about me. You belong in a different world. I have too many responsibilities to even think about a serious commitment. So please forget me."

❧ CHAPTER 4 ❧

*G*inny had gone home first to the brownstone on Park Avenue and then back to Vassar. She never told her parents about Frank, nor had she ever told her aunt. Home seemed the same. She was indifferent, not noticing her mother's efforts to create something beautiful with the newly recovered French provincial furniture.

The first day in Lathrop, the dormitory, she almost forgot about Frank. She and Renée had to run downtown to Luckey's Department Store to buy bedspreads and matching curtains; they tacked a new piece of material over an old, second-hand chair with thumbtacks. Second-hand? It had been in the students' furniture exchange many times. Renée had brought back an electric gadget from Germany so they could make tea in their room and that seemed like a pleasant prospect, even though girls were not supposed to have anything that required electric current. There were books to buy and classes to think about, but mostly it was exciting to see the girls. Betty had a new hairdo and looked dreamy, somehow. That night the three of them sat on the floor in her and Renée's room. Ginny didn't tell them about Frank, she just hinted.

"I told you, didn't I, Betty?" Renée said triumphantly, "Of course, I knew it the minute I saw you, you've had experience. You can tell by looking at a girl that she's had experience!"

"Oh don't be silly," Ginny said.

"Tell us all about it," Renée said.

Ginny shook her head. "Another time, or maybe never, what did you do all summer, Betty?"

"Same old thing," Betty said languidly, and the girls laughed. Ginny felt wise, and old, and pleased with herself that first night. But later, after the semester started, and the classes and the books, and the hard work, and the weather began to get cold, she felt lonely, she felt how artificial a girls' school was, it had nothing to do with real life, she thought, especially with Frank. She wrote to him, and he didn't answer. Instead she had a letter from Emory inviting her to Cambridge for a football game and dance in October. Though Ginny had a long paper due in 18th Century English Lit, she took off for Harvard. She couldn't get up any steam on her studies that year, she wished she'd majored in Economics instead of English, but, of course, she could never do statistics. But she would have understood Frank better then, and also Emory.

The weekend was fuzzy, she cheered madly for Harvard, but they lost. Emory said Minnesota played much better football. She discovered that Emory lived in an apartment with three other business school students, and was surprised that they had no rules about signing in, or women guests, and that even the Harvard dormitories were far more liberal than Vassar's. There were cocktails and a dinner and a dance in one of the houses. Emory didn't want her to dance with anyone else, and he kept talking about his studies and his hobby of collecting butterflies, tropicals that he bought already mounted in New York. She understood that he wanted her to get to know him; he often asked her questions about herself, but she gave him rather short answers. She wasn't sure how close she wanted to be to Emory. She heard a good deal about planned economy and business cycles. She kept thinking of how contemptuous Frank would have been of all these "rich boys" and she longed for his warmth, his weight, and his presence.

Ginny slept late in the odd little room Emory had found for her in a boarding house on Brattle Street. It was up under the eaves with pictures of the landlady's ancestors all over the walls. Emory rang the bell downstairs about 11:00 that morning and the old lady called Ginny.

He was at home in this woman's living room, polite, alert, pleasant, wearing a Brooks Brothers overcoat, very trim. Ginny was wearing a tweed suit with a reefer and hat to match, and she knew she looked as correct as Emory. But she didn't feel correct, and she didn't feel as though Emory was anything special; his conversation bored her sometimes. He was slender, not solid like Frank, and his body didn't interest her. Then she was shocked at herself. Why should his body interest her? She felt guilty. They went to have breakfast at the Copley Plaza Hotel, a long, brunchy sort of breakfast. The dining room was empty and the Black waiters haughty in their uniforms. Ginny's taxi would leave for Vassar at 2:00 in the afternoon, loaded with girls.

Emory leaned forward across the table, "Will you be in New York during Christmas vacation?"

"Sure," she said, "that's home."

"I've decided to stay east then," he said smiling. "Sidney invited me to stay with him and his family. You met Sidney. I want to stay in Cambridge a few extra days to work on my International Trade paper and then I'll come into the city. I've never spent much time in New York, you know. And I hope you'll show me some of the sights of your native city."

"That would be fun," Ginny had said, not really meaning it.

"And there are some marvelous concerts," Emory

said with enthusiasm. "I know you'll love hearing them. And maybe the Met. I haven't seen any opera since I was in high school. I bet you go all the time."

"Not exactly," Ginny said, grinning. "But we'll get together, and I know my parents would enjoy meeting you." "Of course," said Emory, "I want to meet them."

Ye gods, he's serious, Ginny thought all the way home in the cab that she shared with several other girls. I wish I liked him more, she thought, I wish I wasn't just sick for Frank. And then, when she got back to the dormitory that night, Renée was waiting for her. She pulled her into the room, and before Ginny could take her coat off, Renée started, her eyes shining.

"I'm going to get married! At Christmas! I'm quitting school! It's Jacques! He's attached to the French Embassy in Washington now, and he'll be here for simply years and we're going to get married December 20th and go to Florida for our honeymoon."

"Renée! Marvelous!" Ginny shrieked and hugged her.

"And darling," Renée said, "I know you'll be lonesome, but I asked Betty and I think she'd move in with you if you want her, and be your roommate."

And if that were not enough, her major advisor called her in the next day to ask why her work was so poor. Ginny sat in the little cubicle of an office looking at the gray-haired woman in the gray suit that confronted her. Freshman year she'd been afraid of her, and thought she really had a great mind, but now she looked and wondered what it was like to be a single woman and teach in a girls' college. Miss Hartwell had piercing black eyes and she said, "Are you well? Perhaps you should see the doctor?"

Ginny said she was fine.

"Upset about something?" Miss Hartwell asked, "A young man perhaps?"

Ginny felt a hot flush of resentment mounting her cheeks. How she hated blushing so easily. What business was it of Hartwell's? "I've only been away from college two weekends this fall," she said righteously. "One was to go home and finish my dental work."

"Well," said Miss Hartwell, "take your books along during vacation. This is only a warning, but of course we expect majors to get at least a "B" in any English course they take, and your exam was about a C-." She stood up. "I'm sure you'll buck up!" she said, trying to be friendly.

"Buck up," thought Ginny with disgust, "she's really out of the dark ages!"

Ginny left her books in the dormitory when she went home. Betty said the best way to forget one guy was to give another guy a chance. She was sure you couldn't tell by his build what he'd be like. Maybe even more exciting than the first one. Ginny decided it would be easy to give Emory a chance.

Thus, Ginny told me, she'd gone home to New

York, in love with Frank, worried about school, losing her friend Renée. Emory had taken her out, and one evening when they returned, her parents were already in bed. She had then set about to seduce him, knowing by then that he was the kind of man who would marry her, if he slept with her. He fumbled in the darkness, acquitted himself like a man, and then dropped off to sleep, limp and spent. But she felt better than she had since she'd been with Frank.

As I was becoming involved in her story, the boat lurched again and the motor stopped. Ginny leapt up and we both went out on deck. Emory was at the wheel and he was cursing under his breath. He had somehow beached the boat on the shore. He was trying to make it go backwards to get it off the bank and finally asked Sol and Frank each to take an oar and push. With the efforts of the three men we were back in the water. Emory headed the boat toward the channel marker. He announced that we should ignore it; he had been talking with Frank and hadn't watched what he was doing. I was truly alarmed, because I believed that he really was incapable of driving this boat which was taking us all to some unknown fate.

Ultimately Ginny and I returned to the cabin and she returned to her story, which still seemed dramatic. After she slept with Emory, she had lain there in the dark, on the couch, thinking that if Frank owned her, at least she owned Emory, lying there so helpless and vulnerable. And if she got pregnant, it wouldn't matter. He didn't carry safeties in his pocket the way Frank did, but she didn't care. Maybe she'd tell him she was pregnant, but she didn't think she'd have to be that cheap. She could imagine him, his blue eyes holding fear like a dog when you come at it with a roll of paper to spank it, no, she wouldn't have to. She shook him awake and sent him home, and the next morning he called her at 8:00 to ask when he could come to see her father.

She jumped out of bed, shrieked with joy, screamed for her mother, grabbed her in her nightgown and whirled around three times, and then began to laugh. Of course, Emory would be the type to come and see her father! It was a triumph, a victory! To hell with Miss Hartwell! Wait till Renée hears this! She thought, I really will forget Frank now.

Now Ginny sat opposite me and clasped her hands together. "Everybody has a guilty secret, don't they? Why can't I get over feeling guilty about the whole thing? Sometimes I even think I was worse to Frank than I was to Emory, if I hadn't acted like a playgirl, he might have married me. But that's what I am, I guess.

"You know," she said, "I still dream about Frank. And the night we were married I pretended it was Frank, and I've done that ever since. It's crazy, but I can't help it!" Now her face was contorted as she fought off tears and rage and every wrinkle and sign of age she had so successfully hidden appeared as deep grooves of anguish and suffering. I pitied her, as I always pity them, and perhaps that is the only reason I ever succeed, that I have some well of pity to draw from.

"Now you understand!" she said, almost with relief. "Now you know why I need your help. I can't be alone with him! I can't!"

"You needn't be," I said.

"You don't give advice, do you?" she said. "Psychiatrists just listen, don't they, for a fee? I suppose you think I'm some sort of a case now, don't you?" She plucked at the blanket on the bunk. "Do you think I should tell Emory? If Frank and I are both unhappy, he can't be happy with that Aggie, well, people have gotten divorces and married again," but she was shaking her head herself. "The children, of course. That's why I never said anything. I got pregnant right away. How can I be a good mother?"

"That's something different," I said.

She spoke angrily, "Why do I care about Frank when he's let himself get so fat and smokes cigars? I don't let Emory smoke, not since I heard about lung cancer, I guess that shows I want him to live, huh? Why do we get so old so fast? Frank," her eyes were dreamy and far away, "that man out there, he remembers me when I was a girl, I was beautiful, too, and I'm not a girl any more—the wrinkles are coming—and he's old and he's not handsome any more either! And what if he says something or does something to give me away? How could I answer Emory? When I look at Frank I'm just like water inside."

They were shouting to us from the deck. We had arrived at the sandbar. I handed her my handkerchief and she wiped her eyes and took out her lipstick and viciously painted her lips, bright orange-pink. Yes, she had been beautiful as a girl, and she could have been beautiful now, if a serene soul looked out of her eyes, instead of a whining child. I squeezed her hand; it was moist, but surprisingly strong and sinewy. I promised never to tell anyone what she had said. She made her face smile at me, and then turned her back and scampered up the ladder through the door to the deck. Then she turned back. "Thanks," she said.

It would be a long, a twisted process to work with a woman like her, a woman who had built so elaborately, to find out, not why she had slept with a man when she was young, but why she had made it so central to her image of herself. It would take time to discover why she somehow thought because she was guilty, she was also noble, had an interesting secret, how she had used her "sin" to make herself a martyr like some medieval saint, to have sex with one man but always to think of another, to never be satisfied. I was beginning to think American women were more Puritanical than European women, especially about sex.

Perhaps Emory suspected, or even knew she'd had a lover. I've known men who enjoy having a wife with a past, a wife with a secret sadness, a mysterious attractiveness, how superior he would feel if he knew! Especially if Frank still wants her. He too might be proud if he knew. She's still carrying a torch, he'd boast.

I thought how every story is different, how no two humans are alike, how courageous Freud was to look for some common denominator in all of us, even if he failed with individual patients. He opened so many doors for psychiatry and psychology. He invented the talking cure that I truly believe can lead to mature love for a patient. I think there is only one common denominator that matters, mature love, which succeeds where all else fails. A fact as hard to believe as $E = MC^2$, and the major fact in my practice. One of my teachers said, "Life is the greatest psychiatrist," but Ginny's life, her luxurious protected life, how could it give her a sense of reality? And she had a capacity for dramatizing herself.

When I came back on deck, I glanced up at the sky. The day was bright, but gray clouds hung behind the hills on the eastern side of the river. The river was wide here, the sandbar a delta made by a tributary stream. There was a wooded island, looking almost like a barge off to the right, and the hills conical here, too, still reminded me, ominously, of the Rhine. Walter and I had once spent a day on that river, one of our few carefree times together. Really as I look back, I was romantically in love with Walter but yet we hardly had time to know each other. Walter had never known Bill and Bill had never had a father, but Bill was in some ways the only important man in my life. In Italy, I had dreamt that Walter would join us after the war. But that dream had died.

Emory had dropped anchor and cut off the motor. In the sudden stillness, I heard the lapping of water on the hull of the boat, and Frank's voice very loud for a second, "This is great!" and then, as he modulated it to suit the silence, "Not a soul around," he said.

He kidded about getting his bulk into the small rowboat that Emory was now lowering into the water, from a davit that held it at the side of the cruiser. We would leave the cruiser anchored here and row up to the sandy shore in the little boat. Frank took the oars and Aggie watched Ginny and Emory loading the picnic supplies into the small boat. The sandbar extended into the river perhaps two city blocks, and was about a hundred meters wide. There were a few piles of charcoal near the beach, but other than that one seemed to be in wilderness. No house or building was in sight, though when I searched for them I saw the telephone poles lined along the far shore, too small at this distance to see clearly. Emory told us there was a railroad there. It is strange how many places on the American continent give no sign of the hand of man. Maybe that's why Americans make so much noise when they come, I thought, for though there was relief from the noise of the motor, everyone seemed to be talking at once.

Emory handed me down a little ladder into the rowboat; he called it the "tender." Frank had already taken one load ashore, and in a few minutes my foot touched the sand. Suddenly my head felt lighter, as though someone had removed a hat that was heavy and tight. I took off my shoes and stockings and sat there, a little way from the others, feeling the sun-warmed sand under my toes. A little breeze blew against my cheek. The water had an orange cast as it lapped on the shore, and there were a few pebbles at the edge, rounded by the tiny waves. I felt far away from my office and my apartment, I wished my son could be with me, I loved to watch him run and swim, but he was well where he was, I felt calm, as though the world of nature were friendly, as though the hills would receive me with kindness and the waters with peace.

The last load had come ashore now and I stood up and stretched in the sun. Then I went to help Ginny, if I could. Emory was kneeling in the sand building a fire in a special container he had brought along. We didn't have to gather wood for this fire. He had brought fuel and some fluid to make it light quickly, and the whole thing was done in a moment. *Ersatz*, I thought, how could a picnic be real if you didn't go hunting for dead branches in the forest? I was astonished to see that they had even brought along a folding table and chairs, and Ginny and Aggie were setting them up in the sand. Ginny was taking the food out of the boxes and bags, and I helped her spread a tablecloth and put out plastic forks and knives. Emory put steaks on his fire and they smelled delicious. Frank sauntered over to us and put a big hand on Ginny's shoulders. She looked at me as though asking something. "Wonderful spot, and what a feast!" he said. "Tables and chairs, don't we even sit on the ground?"

She shrugged his hand off her shoulder. "You try eating steak with sand blown in it, and you'd be glad we brought the table."

"It wasn't like this in the Boy Scouts," Frank said, laughing. "We ate sitting on the ground with the ants and ate some of them along with our bread and honey."

"Don't worry," I said softly to Ginny when he'd gone over to watch the cooking. I was concerned about her.

❖ CHAPTER 5 ❖

*W*hile we were still eating, Emory said it was such a beautiful day he'd like to stay out longer.

Frank immediately objected "I really need to be back for a light dinner."

"What's so important?" Emory demanded, "daylight lasts a long time in the summer. I'd like to show you Maiden Rock."

"I'd rather get home early; I've got work to do after wasting a whole day."

"Wasting a day?" Emory was astonished. "You call this beautiful cruise wasting a day?"

Aggie interrupted, "He always needs time to work, always, every day."

"Well what about the rest of you?" Emory challenged. Sol shrugged; although I wanted to agree with Frank, it didn't seem my place. Emory announced "We'll go ahead then."

Yet, after we had finished the steaks and salad and potato chips and a delicious pecan pie Ginny had brought, a kind of fellowship and kindness moved among us.

Emory tipped his chair back in the sand and crossed his bare knees. His fine face relaxed and the little wrinkles around his eyes looked like weathering, rather than worrying, he sighed, "I love this place!" He was at home here, as Ginny had said he was at home in the Copley Plaza and in her parents' apartment. Emory was a man who was at home in his world, I thought, and that is an unusual thing, being at home in his own world, he could be at home almost anywhere.

"My dad used to drive us out here when we were kids," he said. "He knew the farmer," Emory waved his arm toward the land from which the sandbar extended. "Anyway, those days, you could hike or picnic almost anywhere, nobody minded if you crossed some barbed wire, (he said 'bob-wire'), so long as you didn't let the cows out. Every spring we came out here. Father knew an old Indian who had a shack down there at the edge of the river, took Dad fishing when he was a boy. He fished and trapped for his living, he'd collect bounties for wolves and rattlesnakes."

Ginny shivered, "You always tell that," she said, "I

don't believe it. Just to scare people."

Emory continued, "At the tops of the hills the wolves may be gone, Virginia, where it's rocky and hot, but there are plenty of rattlesnakes. Even now. They won't bother you unless you bother them."

"Oh, sure," said Frank. "Me, I'd stay off the rocks."

"When I was fourteen, Father let me go hunting with Black John, the Indian," Emory said. "I watched him pin down a snake with a forked stick. He didn't let me get near it, but that was some experience, that snake writhing and whipping its body and rattling and the tongue going lickety-split, and that old Indian mumbling something under his breath and waiting just so long before he came down with the hatchet he held in his other hand. Neat, clean, and ceremonious, only time I ever saw anything else like that was the bullfights in Mexico City."

"When I was fourteen," Frank said, mimicking Emory, "It wasn't animals I had to worry about in my neighborhood, it was the kids. Father let me take a morning paper route in the Italian neighborhood on the west side, in addition to my evening route in the Jewish section. When it was me and one other kid I had a sporting chance, like your friend the snake. One guy could never pin me," he expanded his chest, "When they ganged up on me, I couldn't win. So I had to learn to fight back."

Aggie said, "I never saw the Mississippi River till I was sixteen, even though I lived here all my life.

Then we had a girls' club at the Jewish Center, and they took us to a park in St. Paul for a picnic. We thought it was great." She shrugged. "I don't know. I don't really care so much, I guess nature doesn't send me, you should excuse the expression."

"I'm a city girl, too," Ginny said, "brought up in the Park Avenue slums, and married to a country boy."

"Then I got a job after school in a shoe store," Frank ruminated, "and my grandfather told me he would give me some tips. When he first came to this country he also worked in a shoe emporium, but his English wasn't so good. Half the time he didn't know what the customers wanted. So, he worked out a system. He'd take off the shoe, measure the foot, and then when he went in the back to find his boss to help him get the merchandise, he'd take along his customer's own shoe, that way they couldn't walk out on him. That was his salvation in the new country."

While they were laughing at Frank's story, I remembered my grandmother in a white shirtwaist, with glasses on a black ribbon around her neck, her hair piled high. She did embroidery, and at the same time would sing little songs to me, in a quavering soprano. She would cross her legs, sit me on her foot and sing about a bird who came with a letter in his beak with a message to give Lotte a kiss. Then she would lean forward, kiss me on the forehead and release me. She had been a kindergarten teacher. She used to argue with my mother about Froebel's ideas, and she believed little children were naturally good, if given the proper guidance.

My mind skipped from my own childhood to the little ones in Anna Freud's nursery school, especially the wide-eyed three-year-old boy I had observed so carefully before our seminar in child development. As a beginning psychiatrist, I felt very fortunate to study with her. On my way to America with Bill we spent two weeks in England at Maresfield Gardens, the big house where Anna Freud had brought her father in 1939. When we came she provided care with a German-speaking family for Bill; I had only recently started teaching him English. She had worked with children all during the war and continued now with her nursery school and institute of child development. Anna was Freud's favorite child and appointed successor. When she walked in a room, small though she was, everyone felt her presence. Her piercing blue eyes were the first thing I noticed, and afterwards her wiry body and metallic gray hair. When she sat under her father's large portrait in the living room, one could see that she had the same craggy profile as Papa. Her work with children began with facts about their health, sociological situation, and family relationships. After that she took the analytical approach. I thought that her beginning would be good with adult patients too. Often, a long analysis is not necessary to help a patient. She was a great influence on me. Anna Freud was helpful to me and friendly as well. She called me Lotte.

Lotte I am no more but Charlotte now, and the shadow has fallen between my grandmother and me, between my mother and me, between the 19th century and me, the shadow has fallen between the bright years of childhood and the now gray years, the shadow has fallen, and it has remained, over us, like the gathering clouds, and we don't see clearly any more, but look at each other as though through water, and as though through fluoroscopes, look at each other and see through wavering levels and layers, ever towards the inward person but never sure, for in these shadows and moving living pulsating layers of cells and tissue, nerve and bone, blood vessels, cortices and inward structures, where is the true human? Watching a chest expand and contract under a fluoroscope, is it good or evil? Listening to words, the symbols the nervous system puts forth for its own satisfaction, its own survival, its own protection, listening to layers of words, embroidered like Chinese brocade, decorated and charming, where is the living thought they clothe? What is its meaning? Perhaps, I thought then, good and evil are as irrelevant as the alchemists' formulae for turning lead to gold; if the physicists can throw out causation, then the moralists will soon throw out motivation, and I thought how little joy there was in a boat on the river, or on a sandbar, because we had been swallowed by the 20th century and lay heaving in its acid belly, unable to extricate ourselves.

Frank had gone on about the poverty of his childhood until he had stimulated Sol to speak. It was the warmth in Sol's voice that brought me back to listening. It seemed to me that Frank had been trying to draw Sol into the conversation with his comments about the *shul* his grandfather used to attend. Perhaps Frank had noticed how quiet Sol had been all day.

Sol had explained that his grandfather was an Orthodox rabbi, called to the United States by his *landsleut* (people from his town already in America) to establish a synagogue for them. I noticed that a sweetness and softness had crept into Sol's voice, and I listened to him. He had told how his grandfather had a quaint sense of humor, and a love of learning, how slyly he had questioned him to find out what boys learned in American public schools; how he had a group of men and boys around him who studied Talmud, and how that group dwindled as the years went by, how he conducted high holiday services in his shroud, all white, and how he covered his head with his prayer shawl during those intense moments of personal prayer. He would ask the wealthier members of his congregation to help the poorer; he made a marriage here and found a home for an orphan there; and his congregation always dwindled. I saw that Sol rocked a little as he talked, like a man praying, and how his voice began to take on the inflections of Yiddish. I smiled. I was sure he was unconsciously imitating his grandfather.

Perhaps he heard the Yiddishisms himself, because he also smiled in his one-sided way, the scar looking pale in the bright sunlight, and then said quite abruptly, shifting from *legato* to *andante mobile*, "Well, *kinder*, did I ever tell you how my mother got to this country?"

Ginny got up from the table and sat herself on the sand, leaning her head against Emory's bare knees, and extending her sensuous legs. Emory patted her bright hair half consciously, and then I saw her looking at Frank, as if waiting for a reaction. But Frank was listening to Sol.

"My grandparents had to leave Poland in the summer, so my grandfather could be here on time to conduct high holyday services in the fall. They got their train tickets, and their steamship tickets, and were all ready to go with their children. There was a baby, five months, my uncle Josh, and the four older children, ages about two, four, and seven, and my mother, she was nine years old then. But, when the time came to leave, my mother was sick. I don't know what she had, Grandma always said chickenpox, but her face was quite badly pockmarked and I believe she had smallpox. You know, not too many children survived in those days, my grandmother said that the other women in the village always felt sorry for her because none of her infants died. They believed that since a mother was bound to lose a few of her babies, that she was better off if they died as infants than as children or young adults."

Sol shrugged his bony shoulders. "Well, the family left. My mother was in the care of her grandmother, and they hoped that she could come later, with another family that was planning to travel in the fall. But when their time came, this family couldn't scrape up enough money for their tickets, so my poor little nine-year-old mother left her village all alone to travel to the middle of another continent. The story is she never cried.

"When her grandmother put her on the train, she saw a Jewish woman there and said, 'Watch out for my Hannele.' She had taken some other precautions too, she had sewn money into little Hannah's underclothing, and she had written a tag that she sewed onto the child's coat. 'I am Hannah. I am going to Rabbi Grodinsky, Kansas City, Kansas.' The tag was Yiddish on one side, and on the other, her grandmother had made a day's journey to another town to a clerk who could write English, and he had printed the other side carefully. I know. After my mother died, at the bottom of an old trunk, faded and stained, I found that tag. I wondered how often she might have taken it out and looked at it, her souvenir of her great journey. It's hard for me to imagine how frightened she must have been on that trip.

"Her grandmother had also packed a basket of food for her, bread and cheese, mostly, and admonished her not to eat anything but kosher food.

"On the train, the Jewish woman was friendly, and she was getting off in the city where Hannah was to board the steamship. She walked down to the docks with her in the morning and showed her the boat. Mother told me she didn't mind sitting on the dock and waiting till afternoon till she could board ship, but the sudden blast of the ship's horns frightened her, she thought it was judgment day, or like Mount Sinai when the *shofar* blew and the voice was heard. The stevedores with the big loads frightened her, too. But, after many hours, she went up the gangplank with the other emigrants, ticket in hand, her destination the steerage of the steamship. Inside, there was a terrible rush, each family and each mother trying to make as much desirable space as possible for her own. Yet, after a few hours, a Jewish family noticed her, they told her she could sleep on a blanket they had brought with them, and the mother gave Hannah food from her supply. Hannah helped with the baby because she was used to that. It was smelly and cold in steerage, an Atlantic crossing in the winter, people got seasick and had no adequate way to clean up, steerage passengers weren't even allowed out on the decks, it was miserable. And then Ellis Island. The family that had befriended Mother was held there and she went into New York by herself, but there she was met by a Jewish woman, maybe from Council of Jewish Women. They regularly met Jewish immigrants at Ellis Island. She fed her and put her on the train to Kansas City.

"Now there was no one who understood her language, and this is the part of the story I like best. An old Negro Pullman porter walked through the coaches and saw her. He couldn't talk to her and she couldn't talk to him, but here was a child, he thought, who ought to be playing games, and you know what he did? He taught her to match pennies, and they matched pennies all across the prairies of the United States! When they got to Kansas City, he got off the train with her and told a friend of his, a redcap, to see that she got home. The redcap took her by the hand and walked her the 10 blocks to her father's synagogue, and there he was reciting the evening service when he looked up and saw his own child led by a black man entering the *shul*. He said it was as though an angel had delivered her across the seas."

"Why, I wouldn't any more send a nine-year-old girl all alone from Europe to America, than I would drop a baby in the ocean to see if it could swim," Aggie exclaimed.

I thought of that nine year old and my Bill, eleven when we were in Germany. I remembered Bill's tirade after we had been in St. Paul a few months. "I loved Italy and Maria was so good to me, like a grandmother, and then you took me to Germany and I had to learn German because you were studying, and the kids made fun of me and now I have to learn English and it's the same thing. They tease me because I have a funny accent—you're so busy with your work—I suppose next you'll move to Israel and I'll have to learn Hebrew!" I had determined to spend more time with him after that and we had written to Maria, the marvelous woman who had befriended and then hidden us after the Germans came to Italy. I sent her food packages and money when I could.

I said aloud, "Bill and I were rescued by a wonderful woman named Maria, a midwife who hid us in her little hut so the Germans couldn't find us. I think what she did for us was purely good, even though you might say you can't believe a woman would risk her life to save me and my little boy. It was a great risk because the Italian women came to her hut to be delivered and they knew I was hiding there. Before I was pushed out of the hospital for being Jewish, I had helped Maria with difficult deliveries, but that hardly makes it likely that she would risk so much to hide us."

I wish I could have told Walter about this wonderful person because it seemed as though he, too, owed her something, and he had died as a result of the evil of the Nazi regime, while Bill and I were able to survive.

"It's all too much for me," Aggie said. "Maybe you were rescued by what we call a 'righteous gentile' and Sol, maybe your mother arrived okay; I suppose if you were desperate you could do that today, too. Everybody gets excited about some kid who's fallen in a well or stuck on a mountaintop, don't they? They'll raise money and fly a kid in a private airplane halfway around the world for some special operation or polio cure."

"And, at the same time," remarked Frank, "ignore, or maybe cuss out the slum kids in their own town. When some child gets flown someplace for special surgery, somebody's getting a publicity gimmick out of it, don't worry! Some fund is using it for money-raising; some doctor doesn't mind the boost to his reputation. I don't trust those big stunts at all!"

Ginny spoke about walking down 5th Avenue with her mother, wearing a blue pleated skirt, long stockings, and a middy blouse. She was embarrassed by the ragged children that she knew were Jewish immigrants. I remembered myself, a long-legged child, seven or eight years old. I, too, used to wear pleated navy-blue skirts and white middy blouses and long stockings. One day *Grossmutter* embroidered my initials on the dickey of the middy blouse. I ran to the mirror to look at it, and began to scream with rage, and I can see myself there in the mirror, a long-legged, skinny child with braids flying as I stamped up and down, horrified at what I saw, for my initials were backwards!

Calm and unperturbed, *Grossmutter* appeared in the mirror, her bosom like the prow of some proud ship, and looked down at me with kindly scorn, and waited until I could tell her my trouble.

She made me look down my chin at the offending initials, then stripped the blouse off over my head and showed it to me: the initials were properly written, of course, it was the mirror image that changed right to left and left to right, the mirror image, mirrors are silver now, and it is not right to say "we see in a glass darkly," but when we hold up a mirror to ourselves, there is always this curious reversal. In analysis, it is so hard to get out of ourselves; we can never pull our skin up over our heads and look at it as Grandmother does, with both kindness and scorn, all at once. She had given me a lecture on my temper of course, ending, as she always did, *"Da, siehst du? Siehst du?"* "There, do you see?" That followed me through childhood at the end of every moral lecture, but the mirror is forever reversed, and that is all we have to look in, all the way we have to see.

When I listened again to the conversation on the deck, there was a discussion of Frank and Aggie's daughter Carol. Aggie was complaining that Frank had given Carol her own car. Sol wanted to change the subject so he said his children were young and he wanted to send them to Jewish camps and he wished there was a Jewish day school nearby. I suddenly realized I had no idea what Walter would have thought about Bill's education. I had to make so many decisions by myself.

Emory said he was planning to get his son a car when he started college. Then he ran his hand through his crew cut. "If they have a good education, they'll be okay. Who has a sense of values?" Emory continued, "Look at this river. One hundred fifty years ago, nothing but Indian canoes here. Maybe a French voyageur now and then. A hundred years ago, side-wheelers bringing Swedes and Germans to settle, and lumber mills and little towns wild on Saturday night with lumberjacks, and eighty years ago, the railroad coming through and the river almost deserted. More farmers, when my dad was a boy you might still homestead around here, not the best land, but good enough. All you needed was a mule, or a team of horses, no running water, no electricity, no county agent, you did it with your back and your bare hands. Oxen, some people had, took half a day to go five miles to town. Now we can fly to Florida in that time! None of us would work like that, we're healthier and bigger, but we probably couldn't work like that. I remember Schmidt when he was 84 years old, he was the farmer that owned this land, sitting by an open wood fire, all winter, it seemed like, carving an axe handle. Couldn't do that more elaborate stuff any more, but the way he got that thing smooth, the way he loved its smoothness! All winter long, lovingly working on that one piece of wood, and washing in cold water from the pump, and stomping out to milk the cows twice a day. Now we talk about geriatrics! Now we use the river for recreation and leisure, the world is changing so fast. I like to read local history. In 1872, there was a tremendous accident in the wide part of the river, Lake Pepin, below the locks. The river is shallow but treacherous there. A tremendous storm came up and a side-wheeler capsized. No Coast Guard then, no radio, not even telegraph in this part of the country, that's what really got me! Nobody even knew about this accident until the next day when some Indian child reported to a trader who rushed out there. Forty-two people were drowned!"

"Cheerful thought," Aggie said. Somewhere inside myself, I shivered. My anxiety about this trip did not subside.

Emory continued, "Did I tell you about the rivalry between La Crosse and La Crescent, two little towns across the river from each other, each with a landing? You know, in those days the channel used to shift every year. Mark Twain tells about it in *Life on the Mississippi*, so one year La Crosse would get all the big boats and one year La Crescent would, the two towns were terrible rivals. One year, the good burgers of La Crescent couldn't stand it any longer. They ordered a barge of granite from down river a ways, to build a new courthouse, they said, it came up the river on a dark and stormy night, and strangely enough, sank right in the harbor of La Crosse."

"You and your local history," Ginny said mildly.

"I love this country," Emory said, "I love every rock and hill. I loved it when I was a boy, and I do now, too."

The rabbi stood up and brushed the sand off his slacks.

"Wonderful meal," he said, "not many Jews have a sense of the land the way you do, Emory."

"Not many Jews have lived here as many generations as the Falks," Emory said.

Somehow we all moved toward the shore and stood looking down the river at the clouds moving rapidly across the sky, the wide river, the cliffs in the distance. There was the feeling of width, of vastness, in the landscape that is so typical of the American west, one was not hemmed in by picturesque mountains nor by quaint thatched houses, but one stood on a great river, the Mississippi, that traveled half a continent to the sea, and one felt dwarfed, lonely, and afraid.

Frank put his arm across Sol's shoulder and turned to me, "Here's a great guy," he said, "a sweet guy. He's given up a lot for his temple and nobody bothers to tell him how much we love him."

Sol looked up from under his heavy brows, "Why Frank, you old, so and so, thanks. Thank you very much."

"You deserve it. You deserve a lot more." Frank patted his shoulder and put his arm down, "Watching this guy operate is what brought me back into the fold, you know. So take him for a walk," he told me, "he's the one guy won't ask you for free psychiatry."

"Would you like to?" I asked Sol. I saw that Ginny was busy with putting away picnic things.

"Let's try that path into the woods," Sol said.

❖ CHAPTER 6 ❖

*E*mory and Ginny had started the move for everyone to go waterskiing. Sol and I were not interested, but Frank was eager to try. While they put away the picnic supplies and got out the waterskiing gear, Sol and I walked along the sandbar.

The sand impeded our steps, until we came to the spot where the stream trickled into the river. Stepping-stones had been provided, and we hopped across them, then saw a path leading into the woods. There were oak trees, mostly, interspersed with white pine. The ground was rocky, and I saw little blue harebells by a rock in the sun. We went single file, but some places the path widened out. There was a kind of thick green moss, like miniature pine trees, that looked soft and cool to sit on. I heard birds in the trees, American robins, I thought, and remembered the cuckoo in the forests, in the forests of home, I was almost thinking, but I told myself, "in the forests of Europe," which are more appreciated and better kept than these. Once when it was safe in our Italian hiding place, we hunted mushrooms with Maria. Maria's hair was white and her back was stooped, but her soft brown eyes took in everything. She had a nose for mushrooms, knew all their names and their hiding places. Herbs, too, she knew, even where to find the mandrake. . . . Were her love potions real? Operationally, yes. Her herbs worked quite often, more than chance, almost as often, perhaps, as my kind of medicine works.

She was our Italian angel, Bill's and mine. After they both, my landlord and the hospital, dismissed me because I was a Jew, Maria, the midwife, took us home to her little hut. Why she endangered herself I don't know; probably out of the goodness of her heart. She could still go to the hospital in spite of the Germans. She didn't need me. Bill remembers the rug pulled up and the trapdoor, the moist dark hole we sometimes waited in till the pounding sound of boots above our heads went away, until Maria's sweet voice called us to come up. I tried not to act afraid so Bill wouldn't be frightened, but later he had nightmares about being left in the hole. I did my best to comfort him. I helped with difficult deliveries as I had when Maria had called the hospital. The Italian women knew Bill and I were there but I trusted them not to report us to the authorities because Maria not only delivered their babies and helped with sickness, but was a confidante and a leader for many of them. Still, I was fearful and could almost never let Bill go outdoors. We were prisoners in the hut, dependent on what seemed her never ending kindness.

We were now completely screened from our friends on the sandbar and quite alone. Sol Gordon flopped himself down on one of those beds of moss. "Forgive my silence," he said, looking up at me, his eyes dark under his thick brows, the scar almost hidden from that angle. "I get tired of talk sometimes. I suppose you do, too."

"Yes, indeed." I sat down beside him, and then I lay back.

The moss was soft, but prickly, too, in a strange way, and springy, almost like balsam boughs. I picked up a twig and felt its roughness and looked up at the sky, through all the layers of leaves and branches. The trunk of the tree seemed very tall and very thick, and perhaps because my companion was a rabbi, I thought *aitz chaim*, the tree of life, but a tree is no longer the symbol of strength and majesty it once was, a tree beside the water is strong. We have built bigger things, stronger things; a tree, to a North American, will never be what it was to the Jews of the desert countries: shelter, and even life, because it meant fruit and water. The menorah is "the tree of life." I thought of Jung and I thought he had found too complicated and involved a way to say a simple thing about language and symbolism and our common humanity. Sol was half propped up on his elbows, looking straight ahead, frowning a little.

"I'm not quite at home with these people," he said at last. "They expect me to play a certain role, and I find myself doing it, something halfway between a father figure, who is very wise and omniscient, and some kind of an imbecile who has wonderful high ideals because he really doesn't know what the world is like. Like their own kids that they can't give a sense of reality to, because they have no anchorage themselves," he smiled in his twisted way. "We rabbis aren't prepared to be social workers, or psychiatrists like you, or even administrators. Maybe we have the wrong training: I learned Torah and Talmud, mostly, something about teaching and preaching and writing a sermon, history of the Jews," he paused. "I think about my grandfather often, the rabbi; he saw his community shrink, you know, my congregation is 10 times as big as his, but I have no community. I have in my congregation a few intellectual people, well educated, and intelligent; there are plenty of moral, decent people. There are others who give generously, and who are concerned about the Jewish community in America, and I even have some people who are true Zionists." It sounded like a speech he'd made before, maybe to his fellow rabbis. I stopped listening although he was going on, until I heard something about the counseling he was doing.

"They come to me with all sorts of problems, their marital problems, their home problems. One girl, I hate to say this, one girl in our congregation, seventeen years old, became pregnant last year. The boy wasn't Jewish, I worked with them for a long time."

I had treated the girl's mother after the baby was born and put up for adoption as she and her husband had counseled. But now she was full of anxiety. Should she have raised the child? Of course I couldn't tell him this for professional reasons.

Sol was saying, "I'm tremendously busy, I get many calls to speak from church groups, but I have no community. No group, however small, that truly seeks to live according to Jewish teaching, no group, even, that truly seeks to find the relationship between Jewish life and modern life, even to change tradition to suit modern life. There are a few who are genuinely religious, in any group there are spiritual persons, and artists, and musicians, but they are so stifled, they are so alone, they think of themselves and of God. I am too pragmatic for them, not enough of a mystic, and they are no more interested in the Jewish past than the rest of them. And, because they do not think, their faith is apt to fall apart in a crisis."

"You feel alone," I said.

"Not when I read, not when I study, not when I worship, alone in space, in a way, but not in time, there were others and there will be others, and there was my wife."

I saw tears gathering in his eyes, I saw them brim-ful. His voice dropped to a husky whisper. "Oh it's all a pretense," he said, "of course I'm terribly lonely. My wife is dead, from cancer, and I can't believe it."

I reached out my hand to him, "Oh, my dear," I said. My hand was on his wrist, which was hard and unmoving. I had no words for him, I, a psychiatrist, I, who had lost my husband, my mother and my father and all the rest; I had an unexpected rush of feeling; it has been so long since I touched a man's warm hand. The tears stood in his eyes, but he looked straight ahead, almost consciously trying not to blink. At last he wiped at his eyes with his other wrist. Could anyone have ever said a word of comfort to me in those days? On his face I saw the deep, wordless suffering that I had known, but the other suffering, the suffering that knows, as I knew, even when I counted my dead, that there were six million dead, the suffering that knows that no yachts nor cars nor mansions can keep the man and woman who live within them from the ultimate human reality of death. Without love there is the living death of the neurotic, but with love, oh, when the one you love is dying, after the first anger and the first guilt, there is the suffering that must be endured without any cure, since there is none.

"During the war," Sol's voice trembled, "we lived with death. The men said you never knew whose number was coming up." His thin hand with the tendons and veins standing out touched the scarred cheek. "I got this in the war. I was a chaplain." He shook his head from side to side, "But the years go by, and you lose your sense of the terrible imminence of death. Even I! Even I who preach over the caskets of the dead."

Now the tears came down his lined cheeks, and he looked up, like a Jeremiah, goaded, anguished. "I wasn't a good husband to her, God knows. God knows I left her alone night after night for meetings, classes, groups, and for what, for what?" He shook his head, slowly again, and ran his hand through his coarse, dark hair. "There were times when I thought God called me to this job, to teach, to lead, to serve, my God, what illusions we create for ourselves! And all the time I forgot the most elementary thing, the very beginning of all that's holy, to live with my own wife in peace and in love. I put her aside. She didn't speak to me toward the last and I couldn't speak to her. Once, when I tried, she said, "Go and pray." His voice was grating, holding back sobs. "I can't pray now."

"You'll pray again," I said, "and I know what you also know, that guilt always overwhelms one after the death of someone one loves."

"I know! I know! And I am more guilty than them all!" He rose to his feet and shook his fist at the sky. "I sought community! Community with men of faith! And I turned my back on the only community that was available to me, the community with my wife!" He stood, looking down at me, "She was a woman of faith and sweetness, and understanding." Then he looked away, "and she wasn't afraid, when she first knew she had cancer, she wondered how I was going to manage the children, sometimes she talked about it as matter-of-factly as a railroad timetable, because I hadn't been home much with them."

"But you still . . ."

"Why didn't I learn from my religion?" he said, "Why didn't I remember how we all stand in danger of death, how precarious life is; why didn't I remember to build a peace, not with God, but with her? With her! And my children, with them there is hope. How did I set aside the immediate, crying need of my own wife, yes, and at first, when we came here, and the babies were small, once she did cry because I was going out on synagogue business—committees, meetings, for the tenth night in a row. How could anything have seemed bigger? The world was created for her, why didn't I remember that *midrash*?"

"For her?"

"For each one of us, alone, singly" he said quietly as he once more sank to the green moss. "There is a teaching that if a life is destroyed, a world is destroyed that, therefore, this world was created for each one of us. Not for the Jewish people or for the glory of God. For you. For me. For her." He rocked his body back and forth, half sobbing, "Why didn't I learn? Why didn't I? Why didn't I learn?"

In spite of myself, I knelt beside him and took his head in my arms and I kissed his hard damp forehead, and I stroked his coarse hair, and I remembered my husband, Walter, and I wept, and my tears fell into his hair. It was as though all the books were closing, closing, and only my heart was left, beating, exposed, and Sol responded to me. He drew me down to sit there, and put his arms around me, and my face came into his bony shoulder, and he kissed my cheek, and he was comforted. We half lay there, on the moss, and his breathing quieted so that I heard a squirrel chattering like an angry little alarm clock far up in some tree. I heard wind sighing through the branches and felt the sky darkening again as the sun went behind another gray cloud. Unsettled weather, I thought, unsettled like us.

After a little while, without more words, we began to walk slowly back toward the sandbar. Before we had left the woods, we heard angry voices, Frank and Emory's. Sol and I stopped. We couldn't hear it all, but Emory was saying, "He's gone to all lengths," then something about the Mexican government and an antiquity. "You can't change that plan now!"

"Hell, this isn't an art gallery, it's a shopping center!" Frank shouted loudly. Sol put his hand on my arm to prevent me from moving forward.

Emory responded so quietly I couldn't hear his reply, but then I heard Frank's voice, loud again, "Buy me out? Now? Boy, you've got rocks in your head. I don't give a damn," and then his voice faded. Sol pulled me forward a step and we could see them now through a gap in the trees, their backs to us, walking along the sand toward the boat, Frank swinging his shoulders angrily while Emory put up a hand to touch Frank's back. Segal shrugged him off. "Everybody's got troubles," I said to Sol, trying to smile, "What do you suppose that's all about?"

"Well, I knew Emory and his company were involved in planning a new shopping center. There was a big spread in the paper last Sunday. I didn't know that Frank had anything to do with it, but I suppose a lot of people work on a big project like that. Let's go back, shall we?"

Frank said "your charm and art gallery will cost us millions every year. We need more than two anchor stores; we need to please them. They won't change their way of doing business because you want to be charming."

Emory dismissed Frank's complaints, saying, "In the long run, we'll make more money."

Frank loudly retorted, "You've always had money! We had to work for it." Emory noted that Frank had changed from an idealist to caring only about the bottom line.

We came back to find the two women in their swimming suits; Frank and Emory were on the boat. The waterskiing had begun. No one seemed to realize there had been sharp words, or even sad ones. Ginny chattered on in her brittle way and Aggie stood there, her superb figure insolent in its brief covering. When the men emerged, they ferried me out to the cruiser so I could change.

Since childhood, I have loved to swim. First I learned the breast stroke, with my head high in the water, but now I swim any way, side stroke or crawl, or underwater. I walked into the cold, flowing river. I swam out and then turned down, down, opening my eyes in the orange water, seeing reeds before me, swaying slow and easy, wash me, oh river, eternal river, changing river, take me, make me clean of all who cling to me, leaving with me the soil of their souls and their lips, their confessions of weakness and sinfulness. It seemed to me that I could stay there forever, underwater, swaying slowly, weightless, as though the weight of guilt was truly floating away from me, down the river, I submerged, silent, free, there was a moment like the climax of love, but cool, a moment all floating, all feeling, and then, against my will, as the climax subsides against one's will, I came to the surface to gasp, to breathe the thin and searing atmosphere in which we have our being.

Now I saw that the clouds were piling up, towering, and I observed the hills, wooded mostly, but some of the rock bare and steep, glacial hills, ancient, ancient. Emory was at the controls of his boat, and Frank was going to water-ski. I swam along easily, watching them, Frank crouched deep in water, awkward, the tips of skis in front of him; they yelled back and forth. Suddenly, Emory opened the throttle, the motor roared, Frank jerked up into the air, spray flying, still crouched, then slowly stood erect, rope in hands, skiing over the foam in the wake of the boat. Frank is a big man, but out there on the broad river in the increasing distance, he looked terribly small, frail, in peril. His life seemed to me held as though in an eggshell, between water and sky, moving at great speed behind the roaring boat. But then I tried to tell myself: ridiculous fantasy, it's only a sport with a small element of danger, just enough to make it sporting, really, it was a day of premonitions and speeches to myself. Of warnings I would not hear, because I wouldn't close the books, I wouldn't trust my own intuition speaking to me of danger.

I dove deep into the water again, but it was not the same, and I surfaced rather quickly, almost with a feeling of panic, to see Aggie motioning to me from shore and shouting, "Come back in, you're too far out." I hadn't noticed, after all, and turned toward her. She had told us she couldn't swim.

❧ Chapter 7 ❧

*A*ggie glanced at me sideways, the planes of her face so bared of flesh I thought of the death's heads in the medieval figures of the danse macabre on the cathedral when I was a little girl. I used to make a wide detour around the cathedral if my nurse ever walked me that way. And yet this did not come to me as an omen, I only remembered afterwards that I had seen death looking out of her dark eyes and her skeletal face.

"She doesn't like me," Aggie said, and the word "she" was almost a hiss, "I don't know what it is, maybe she's just a snob, maybe it's something more, my son Robert once asked her daughter to a dance and the girl said her mother made her refuse. It's just as well; those two girls are so spoiled. Robert is too sensitive to be flung to a girl like that and be hurt, she's so used to taking all the time, never giving, and she doesn't even know she's doing it. Even when she volunteers at the hospital, even when she tries to work, she doesn't know how, she expects the other girls to do things for her, and they do, too. Of course she's pretty."

I spoke with the mild voice of logic. "But Ginny invited you for the day," I said. "She must enjoy your company."

"Don't be ridiculous! It's the men. Of course, they've got a business deal to discuss. I don't think she knows it; they've been working on this shopping center for months now. You must have seen the write-up in last Sunday's paper."

I recalled it, because Sol had reminded me earlier. There had been a picture of Emory and some architect's drawings of the new shopping center, and the architect was a man I knew, Gunther Neumann. He had been trained at the Bauhaus, and he had left Germany in 1936 to work on some great government buildings in Brazil. He built apartment buildings on stilts in Cleveland one year, and a municipal auditorium shaped like half a grapefruit in some California town another year. Now he was about to create a shopping center "with the atmosphere of a sleepy Mexican *zócolo*, or village square, where one can walk at leisure and see the wares displayed by the natives." He had been in Mexico lately and, to capture the Mexican climate, the whole thing would be glassed in and one of the famous muralists would come and paint a wall somewhere, the only one that wasn't glass.

"I didn't see anything about Frank in the write-up," I said.

"No," she said, "he says he's the silent partner, let Emory get the credit, but he'll make money, only something's gone wrong. He's spent a tremendous amount of his time on this shopping center, I know that, and I know now he's very worried about it."

Frank was out on the river driving the boat while Emory jumped over the wake on his water-skis, a little like a hound after a mechanical rabbit, jumping, jumping, and never catching up.

"You see," Aggie said, digging her long fingers into the sand, "I'm not an educated woman. Not like Ginny, with her art and all. I've heard of impressionists, but who was that other one she mentioned?"

"Jackson Pollack?" I said, "He's an American. I don't know a lot more than that."

"I'm always behind," Aggie said, "I never catch up. Frank is always ahead of me somehow, I guess he knew about that artist. Or else it didn't bother him. Robert, our son, you know, is interested in art. He wants to major in it, it seems so impractical to me, and Frank says it's okay. I don't understand why Frank wants to do business with people like the Falks, they're so rich and society and all, and educated, the women at the hospital say Ginny's a fake, she's more interested in men than culture and art. I can't even judge, how would I know? She knows more about it than I do. The way I look at it, the Falks have no place to go but down. And if something goes wrong with this deal, then Frank would get all the blame."

"I don't see that," I said.

"He's always a big hero, you know," Aggie said, smiling rather fondly, "Frank, I mean. He's restless and he changed from one thing to another, labor law first, and then the war, and then private practice, and now he's hardly practicing law at all, he's in business really. We're going to have to invite these people to our house, and I don't know how to give a party that she would like."

"What do you mean, he's always a big hero?" I asked. And once more I knew I was going to listen to a personal story.

"I think that's even why he married me," Aggie said, "because I needed him so badly. If you ask him, he'd wink and say I had the best build at North High or something. But that wasn't quite it. You see, we'd been going together a little when my father died, he was working his way through law school then," Aggie began to tell me about her life, "back in the '30s," as she said. "After Dad died was when Frank really got serious," she explained.

"When I first knew Frank, he was a fighter. He was mad and he was a fighter. I was mad then, too, but not the same way, angry all the time, really, sullen because I felt so trapped, so cheated. We used to live upstairs of a grocery store and tailor shop. My Dad had the shop for a long time, then he got sick and had to give it up. You went in the back door by the alley and up some wooden steps. Well, it was a hole we lived in. Dad and Mother had the bedroom and I slept in the so-called living room on a studio couch with broken springs. I hated it every night when I came home to it and every day when I left. When I was a little girl, Dad used to brag about the land of opportunity and all that, and, by the time I graduated high school, I was working for fifteen dollars and fifty cents a week and all three of us had to live on it, he couldn't do tailoring any more. And then, even though things were so terrible, they got worse."

She described how she'd gotten off the streetcar one afternoon after work and found a little group of people in front of the grocery store. There was a policeman standing there and one of the neighbors nodded toward Aggie.

"You live upstairs?" he asked her.

"Yes," she said, suspicious, frightened, angry.

"Old man had a heart attack," he said, "they took him in the ambulance. The doctor's up there with the old lady." Aggie rushed up the stairs and threw open the door.

Her mother lay on the couch, crying, wailing really, wringing her hands, pushing at the young intern as though to push him away. He turned and looked at Aggie. "You the daughter?"

She nodded. He looked at her coolly, estimating

whether she'd begin to cry, too. She stood quite still. He took her arm, his hand was cold, and pulled her into the kitchen, where Dad's sewing machine was set up on the table, "She doesn't know it," he spoke very low, "it was a heart attack. The old man's your father? She thinks we took him to the hospital," he shook his head. "Well I'm sorry to tell you, he's at the county morgue." Aggie couldn't speak. He went on, "I've already given her a sedative, she keeps on yelling, but she's calming down now. I'll go back with the officer if you can handle her."

Numb, silent, she nodded again, then spoke, "What do I do when the sedative wears off?" she asked. He wrote her a prescription and left it on the table and walked out.

Aggie stood over her mother, who looked up with recognition in her eyes, then turned toward the wall and began to scream again. Aggie went into the kitchen and then returned. "Mother," she said. The woman quieted down a little, sobbing, her body shaking, but still not looking. At last she said, "He told me last week, the week before, pains in the chest, I told him to go to the doctor. He said forget it, no money for doctors, and now! Now!"

"Why didn't you tell me?" Aggie said.

"You? What could you do?" Yes, what could she have done? There was no money for doctors.

Her mother sat up, her cheeks were wet with tears and her gray hair had pulled out of the bun and lay every which way on her cheeks and down to her collar. "And now, how do we pay for the hospital?"

Aggie shook her head. "No, Mother," she said, "not the hospital."

"Not the hospital? What are you saying?"

"That's what the doctor told me, Mother, not the hospital, the funeral parlor."

Her mother's shriek rose into the air and hung there, like a living thing, vibrating. Then she began to rock herself and cry, and it was a new crying now, more rhythmical as though it would last forever.

Aggie thought she'd get her mother's sister, her Aunt Polly, and she opened the door. The Levinsky kid was standing there in the hall, wide-eyed. She gave him a nickel, "To get Mrs. Schwartz," she said.

"Schwartz?"

"Yeah, you know, on Newton, up a block and a half from the bakery, on the third floor. She's my aunt, tell her her sister needs her."

"Okay," the kid said, and turned on his heels and ran down the dark steps.

"Polly's coming," Aggie told her mother, "Polly's coming, Mother."

Only wailing answered her.

After the funeral, they moved in with Aunt Polly and Uncle Morris because it was the only way they could pay back the undertakers. It was a gray, unpainted frame duplex. Aggie had to share a bedroom with her mother, who tossed and cried herself to sleep every night and then snored. The window opened on an alley where the garbage cans were never covered. Uncle Morris wandered around in carpet slippers in the evening, snapping his suspenders and asking Aggie why she didn't find maybe a nice young fellow, she should get married. Aggie had written a note to Frank saying she was moving, but night after night, she wondered if his mother had kept it for him until he came home from the lumber camp where he was working that summer and, if he had it, or whether he'd never get it. One day after work, she wandered over to her old house and found the Levinsky kid.

"Has anybody been around here asking for me?" she said.

He shrugged his shoulders, then looked up, shrewd, "Been expecting your boy friend?" he opened his mouth and laughed like a horse.

Hoping she wasn't blushing, she went to Mrs. Levinsky with a story about the insurance adjustor she was expecting. "No, I don't think so," her old neighbor said, "If anyone asks for you I'll tell them where you are."

Uncle Morris insisted on her going to the synagogue for the holidays that year. He said she must stand up and say *kaddish*, after all, her father had had no son. When her mother heard that, she wailed again. Polly would say, "Now, sister, tch tch tch," and Mother would pay no attention.

The synagogue was small and old, and needed paint, like her uncle's place. Aggie went, heard the cantor's trembling voice, and thought, Jews, we can stay home and cry by ourselves, why come here and do it in Hebrew? She felt the tears running down her cheeks, and tried to tell herself that she was better off than her ancestors had been, in the filthy alleys of Europe, and was unconvinced. She knew if she could pray she'd pray for all the things she wanted, she stood up and mumbled the words and sat down again, and looked at her mother, and saw that her face was relaxed, smoothed out, quiet, almost peaceful, and wondered.

It was one evening in the middle of October when their buzzer sounded. Uncle Morris went downstairs and then yelled up so all their neighbors could hear, "Aggie, a young man for you!"

She thought suddenly, wildly, where will we go? Not in the living room with Polly and Morris and Mother! Not in our bedroom! And it's too cold outside, why had she wanted him to call at all? There was no place for them.

Frank stood at the living room door now, Uncle Morris was showing him in, welcoming him to "our little place." Frank wore a white shirt, marvelously clean, his chest was bigger, his grin wider than she remembered, he reached out his hand to her, and gripped hers hard, "I couldn't find you," he said. "That woman at your building kept saying she didn't know where you had gone, I called your office, they didn't know either."

"Called my office!"

"They wouldn't call you to the phone of course, I

said I was an insurance adjustor (they'd both used the same excuse!), they just said no information."

"That Mrs. Levinsky, I'll kill her!"

"My brother-in-law saw you at *shul* with your Uncle Morris, that's how I figured I'd come over here."

"I'm so glad!" Aggie said, "So glad!" Frank looked so big and warm, so young, so kindly, he talked to them all and she couldn't even hear the words, just being conscious of his warmth and the way he was kind and light-hearted with everybody, even her mother, and looking at the smiles on their faces. Smiles! When had there been smiles last?

"A glass of tea?" Aunt Polly was all ready to bustle in the kitchen.

But Frank said he'd come to take Agnes out, and he led her away from them downstairs. Most of their dates were in the park that winter. He never talked about getting married and Aggie said she wouldn't have believed him if he had. Marriage might have rescued her from her desperate situation, she just didn't know if Frank was the hero who might save her.

Early that spring, he showed her with great pride a beat-up Pontiac that he had bought all for himself. He told her how he loved her family because they were good, working-class Jews, decent people, work hard all their lives, don't expect much, but he was going to see that they got more, he'd passed his bar exams! They were going to celebrate! At first, when they drove up to the restaurant, she was embarrassed, she wasn't really dressed for it, but she rode on the wave of Frank's ambitions and pleasures and forgot herself and laughed and loved him when he ordered cocktails and loved him when he joked with the waiter as though they were comrades.

Finally, he found a job at $25 a week as a law clerk in a firm that was specializing in labor law. After dinner one evening, he and Aggie drove slowly out of town. He couldn't get the heater to work when the car stopped, so he had to keep driving.

"Aggie," he said, one hand on the wheel, one arm across her shoulders, "let's get married!"

"Oh Frank!"

Somebody tooted at them from behind and he said, "Goddamn!" and pulled up to the side of the road and turned around and kissed her, hard. The motor died and the heat went off. "How about next week?" he said.

"Next week!"

"Sure, what's there to wait for? We're not going to have any fancy wedding, are we? It only takes three days to get the license."

"Frank, I've got my mother to take care of, and bills to pay from my father's funeral."

"I know. Look. My sister was engaged for five years, did you know that? For financial reasons. Finally she married the guy, but she got so shriveled and dried up waiting all that time, she's just a shrew, really! She nags and screams, she waited too long.

Hell! I can't wait till the messiah comes, neither can you! So, you'll keep on working and give money to your mother. We can live on what I make. I have to help out at home sometimes, too."

"Frank, I don't know how we can."

"Look, you know something? I'm a good cook, marry me and be well fed, as long as you work, I'll help you, really I will, women gotta have rights too, you know, working-class women!"

"What about kids, Frank, we might . . ."

"So we'll wait a couple of years to have kids, is that so terrible? Honey?"

Her teeth were chattering. She felt herself shaking all over.

He took her in his arms, "I love you, I love you, Silly!" his mouth so close to hers, she felt the warmth of his breath on her lips. "Say yes! Right now!"

"Yes, all right," she said. "My God, I gotta say yes so you'll turn on the heater again!"

He roared his laughter and triumph and started the car with a lurch. The heat began to float around her feet. She was still shaking.

"Next week?"

She said, "Give me a little time, then Mother can write to all her relatives and everything, it won't look like a shotgun deal."

"Or a *shadchen* deal?" he chuckled at his own pun. A *shadchen* is a matchmaker.

Aggie began to be happy about planning her wedding; she said she'd never known she had a good figure until Frank told her so. They had set a date and rented a one-room apartment over a bakery, and the weather suddenly turned hot as it sometimes does in Minnesota early in the summer.

Frank met her one evening in high spirits. "I think it'll be a real strike!" he said as they walked toward North Common together.

"What are you so happy about? Real strike? What strike?" she asked, alarmed.

"Haven't you been reading the papers, Ag? The truck strike."

"The truck strike," I watched Aggie as she stood up now, stretched tall in her bathing suit, and looked down at me. "How could I tell you about it?" she said, "How could you understand how excited Frank was, how thrilled really, to be into this thing. He was so thrilled and excited about that damn truckers' strike he actually put off our wedding day. I lost my job because the only way I could ever see him was to work down at strike headquarters on that miserable labor sheet they published. Typing. You know he even went to jail! My poor mother, how she cried." Aggie sat down again. "You know what they struck for? Forty-two and a half cents an hour and the right to organize. They were getting forty cents an hour then. A raise of less than three pennies. The right to organize. My God, I thought I was marrying a maniac. But Frank thought this strike would change the way workers were treated. There would be laws guaranteeing workers' rights to organize and to strike. Meanwhile in the midst of a hot summer, no trucks were delivering food or ice; they made an exception to supplies for hospitals. The employers were organized, a group called the Citizens' Alliance, and they were powerful.

"I thought I'd known Frank all my life and that he was unhinged. He was a fury, down there day and night, writing editorials for that paper, delivering fiery speeches, in secret conference with the governor, like I said, a hero. Gave up getting married for that strike. And I remember the heat. It was like being sick it was so hot, 98 and 100, and even 105 degrees. No trucks, no ice deliveries. People with cars could go get their own ice from the icehouses where it was stacked up, covered with sawdust, milk turned sour in five minutes. And the heat added to the violence between the police and the strikers. The governor called out the National Guard, but you know what bothered me most? The wind, the wind began to blow and that fine dust came at us, all the dust off the Dakotas, you'd get it in your teeth and your eyes, your food, even in your bed at night, I told Frank God didn't want the strike. He got terribly angry. I said this wasn't a climate for human beings to live in. He got even angrier. He got so furious he left and went down to union headquarters, it was an old garage on Second Avenue. Well, then, I went home and there was mother weeping, and my aunt and uncle complaining, and I hated it. I had to get out of there. I went down to union headquarters and helped again. Frank didn't believe me when I said I didn't care if they won or lost, he thought my heart was in it."

Her eyes looked out over the river. "I didn't understand him then, and I don't understand him now. Why does he want to do business with this Falk?"

Ginny was water-skiing now, making wide arcs to one side of the boat and then to the other. Aggie motioned toward her, "I can't do things like that," she said, "but Frank married me anyway, finally, I think the summer before Dad died he was going out with some rich girl, (yes, I thought), but he wouldn't marry for money, he wouldn't even marry a girl he was in love with, if she had money, he said. He had to find a girl who needed him. Like me. When we first got married, he used to read to me out loud, history and philosophy and stuff like that, then the war came, and he had to be a hero by enlisting in the Navy. Robert was born while he was in the service, and then Carol.

"We argue about the children, how would I know how to bring up rich kids? I was poor. I tell Carol to mend a sock and he says, 'Forget it, we threw them away in the Navy.' Sometimes I think he loves her more than he loves me, but he's always giving me things, too. I thought Robert should earn some of his spending money while he was at Harvard, but Frank said, 'Forget it, let him study!' Now he wants to send Robert to Europe for a year to study art as soon as he gets his degree. On his dad's money. When do these kids ever get independent? I mean, financially. In a way, it was probably simpler to raise kids when you were poor."

The boat was coming toward us now, heading in as though it would hit the shore, when suddenly it swerved and stopped, rolling sideways in the waves. Ginny had sunk into the water slowly and was swimming toward us.

When Frank came up to us, I smiled at him, "Why'd you marry her?" I asked.

"Why, she was the Venus of the Vurking classes," he said. "Weren't you doll? Most gorgeous girl that ever went to the Talmud Torah," he tousled her hair. "Come a long way, haven't you?"

"With my rich and famous husband," she said.

"You know why she married me?" Frank asked. I shook my head. "To get away from Aunt Polly and Uncle Morris and Mama, and maybe because she likes it a teeny-weeny bit sometimes, don't you?"

"Frank!" Aggie threw a handful of sand at his legs and said, "Shut up!" and got to her feet.

❖ CHAPTER 8 ❖

*F*inally we were chugging along and after swimming and eating I was sleepy and relaxed. There was some quiet talk until I heard a loud exclamation from Emory who was piloting the boat. I looked at the shore and saw a young man frantically waving his arms and shouting. There was a small boat beached beside him and it seemed that there was someone lying on the ground. We were too far to see clearly.

Emory turned toward the shore while everyone tried to see what was happening. Soon we could hear the cries for help. As we approached I saw that the man lying on the beach was injured. Blood covered his head and part of his upper body. As I recalled that our boat couldn't get all the way to the shore, I removed my shoes and went to the cabin to get clean towels and I wet one. Emory was now close to shore and the young man had stopped waving his arms, only pointing to the man on the beach. As I had expected, we couldn't get closer to the beach because the water was too shallow. I jumped in and waded as quickly as I could. After beginning to clean the blood from the man's face, I saw his forehead had a jagged gash, ten or eleven centimeters long; I put pressure on it to slow the bleeding, but it didn't stop. An old medical school joke flitted through my mind: if the head is bleeding, put the tourniquet on the neck. He was unconscious, breathing unevenly. With my left hand I opened his mouth, no water, only a few weeds that I pulled out. I continued the pressure and checked that there was no other source of bleeding.

"Get me a needle and thread, a box of matches, and blankets," I commanded, looking up at the people on the boat. "And you'd better call the coast guard or whoever can get him to the hospital." My patient was a white male adolescent; his age would help him recover. His friend, dancing up and down, kept asking "Is he okay, will he make it?" I tried to encourage him without promising anything and asked him his name. He said he was Tom and his friend's name was Bucky. I sterilized the needle in the flame of the match, threaded it and began to stitch up the wound. It was many years since I had done this procedure, but it came as easily as many other skills, lodged not only in the brain but even in the fingertips, a kind of kinesthetic memory. As I drew the skin together the bleeding slowed and when I finished there was only an ooze. I wrapped him in blankets and sat back on my haunches thinking about his continued unconsciousness. Tom told me that Bucky had dived off the boat in what they both thought was deep water, not realizing there were large rocks underneath. Tom had pulled him into the boat. By now the rest of my group had come ashore. Soon we heard sirens and a tall grey ship, I supposed the coast guard, came into view. It had many masts, or perhaps communication equipment sticking up. In what seemed a short time a uniformed man was looking at my patient. He complimented me on my stitching.

"You must be a good dressmaker," he said. I merely answered that I was a doctor. He looked surprised.

Now that my responsibility was over, I began to shake. The boy was being carried on a gurney to the grey ship, but I remembered Tom and asked if he could go too. The officer wasn't enthusiastic but agreed, possibly because of my new authority as a doctor. Tom said he and his father could pick up the rowboat later.

Back on Emory's cruiser, I was surrounded, congratulated, admired. I told them I had done what any doctor would have done. The real hero was Tom, who had pulled his friend into the boat, gotten him ashore, and signaled for help. It was lucky we had come along when we did and turned in to investigate. After a while when things calmed down, I realized I had acted as a doctor almost mechanically, thinking only about the immediate problem. But now I was again infused with thoughts of how dangerous boating could be, wondering if our endless journey would be without crises of its own. And if I, or anyone else, would be able to deal with whatever might happen.

Frank asked Emory, "What would you have done without Charlotte? Water is not exactly a natural environment for human beings." I didn't hear Emory's response, but I realized that he made piloting a boat look easy, but one didn't know who was really in control on the river.

We were all settled back on the cruiser. If my husband were here, I could have appealed to him to tell the other men I wanted to go home. I might have succeeded. But I am a wife without a husband. No mists of time obscure his image; he stands in the railroad station in Berlin in August 1939, waving at me as I leave for Italy. I have discovered I am pregnant. He is sending me to safety. He takes the pipe out of his mouth to wave it at me and to smile. Walter, Walter, his name repeats itself. I am alone.

I am used to thinking of my patients as individuals, not as members of families or groups, but now I am making a journey with a group of people, two women who have told me a little of what they see in the mirror when they look in it, one man who has also spoken to me, and two who have not, yet they are revealed as they speak, as they act, as their wives speak and act. A scar, a gesture, a joke reveals what they think they have hidden: they are not young, carefree, wealthy Americans, they are middle-aged, worried, afraid; they fear the loss of such wealth as they have. They are Americans, but they are also Jews.

❧ CHAPTER 9 ❧

I followed Ginny mechanically back to the cruiser and we changed into our dry clothes in the cabin while the men waited. I think what we have lost is not only our prayer shawls, our stooped backs, our ragged clothes. We have exchanged these for the outward and visible signs of prosperity, but what do cars, fine suits, even white T-shirts and soft-soled gum shoes, have to say of the inward and spiritual reality? The rabbi frowns, or does he scowl? The businessman chain-smokes, the attorney bites his nails, and restlessly paces about the boat. We have forgotten some languages, we have not learned the new speech of art, and we have forgotten the simple language of dream and image and symbol, we have analyzed the whole, which is greater than its parts and found the parts, and lost the whole. We do not speak to each other; we do not speak to our inward selves, and the inward self, dry and discontent, itches in us, irritates us, will not be still.

I see Sol at an odd angle and for a second he looks like Walter. The last time I saw my husband, at the railroad station in Berlin, Walter, Walter, waving goodbye to me and to our unborn child. And, because I have thought of Walter in the Berlin railroad station, why not at home? Why not at the hospital where we both studied and worked?

Now my mind goes down its well-worn groove of horror to the other thing that happened the day I left Berlin, at the German border. My papers were in order. I carried nothing except what was allowed. When the train was stopped at the border, the customs officer looked at my bags and initialed my passport. But he was followed by an SS officer who ordered me into the station. I cannot remember this man's face; all I can remember is that he was huge and that he had muscular hands with dirty fingernails. He shoved me into a room where three other SS men, one quite young, were lounging against a table. They straightened up as he came in. The room was glaringly lit, and on the wooden table were stains, stains that my hospital training told me were bloodstains.

"Some people have smuggled out diamonds," said the SS officer, "especially women. We will permit nothing to leave the Reich!" He ordered me to sit on the table and to undress. I was shaking; blood, perhaps this was the end after all. Walter. Walter had arranged everything, he had one more mission to complete for his Resistance work and then he would join me; that was our plan and that was the mission which was never completed, the mission in which they caught and killed him and the others, probably torturing them first. I was shivering. But now, oddly, I thought, what will he do if I'm not safe, waiting for him? I felt terribly embarrassed to remove my clothes in front of these men and the SS man grabbed my head and ran his rough hands through my hair and behind my ears, made me open my mouth, and pushed his thumb against my nostrils.

"Everything off!" he ordered, and when my clothes were all in a little heap, I put my hands over my breasts to hide them. He ordered me, "Lie down!" As I did so, two of the men came at me, grabbed my bare legs, pulled them apart and bent my knees so violently my heels touched my buttocks. The third man thrust his hand in my face so I couldn't scream, while the captain, with his dirty fingernails, roughly, painfully, thrust his hands in me, into my genitals, pulling me apart, saying coldly, "Here is where they hide diamonds! Here! Here!" His hands burning and twisting and tearing inside of me. And I so fearful he would cause me to miscarry!

And then they were all laughing. "*Heraus!*" the officer ordered. "Go back to the train, and don't come back to Germany!" They laughed while I struggled to get into my clothes, while I shook and shivered and sweated and sobbed, as I did for hours, so afraid they had hurt my child, Walter's child. Sometimes it is as though I never got up again, I am forever burning in that awful pain, naked, shamed, utterly helpless. I am forever alone.

Long afterwards, after my son was born, after the war, I returned to Germany to finish my psychiatric training. Not by choice, but because I was sent there. The Allies required Italian and German universities to give surviving Jewish students free tuition. The Joint Distribution Committee, the Jewish agency that collects money from some Jews to help other Jews, the very fund the men were talking about earlier that day, provided room and board. In 1946 they helped me study in Munich; now they send Moroccan Jews to study in Israel, and, of course, do a great deal more besides. It was miserable being in the country that had murdered Walter and the rest of my family, yet the language and the culture were familiar. I wanted to finish as soon as possible.

Not long afterwards I told my analyst about how the border guards had frightened and humiliated me when I left Germany. We sat in his office at the University in Munich. He was a middle-aged Viennese, my doctor—not a Jew, but once a socialist, and he had been interred in a labor camp. We were talking across his desk that day. He was tired and rested his head in his hands. But now he looked up, his brown eyes focused directly on me. He spoke slowly. "Well, you are schooled in self-observation," he had said. "Now perhaps you will tell me. Do you remember this incident, dwell on it, because you are, perhaps, after all, a masochist? You perhaps, after all, received some stimulation that you wanted?"

I looked at him coolly, I thought of his remark numbly, objectively, and I shook my head. "No, I don't think so," I said.

"Ahh," he said, rather quietly. He waited for me to say more, but I said nothing. He went on, "Very well, had you been masochistic I believe you would have become very angry at my suggestion. I think after all it was the shock, the trauma, what so many of us experienced, taught to respect our officials and to obey our codes of law, and then experiencing a paralysis of the will when we found them breaking some law of society which we thought they upheld."

I shook my head. "No," I said. "I remember because I am ashamed of my own shame. I was degraded. I was nude in front of four clothed men. I was psychologically raped. And all my childhood training and adult experience made me feel terribly ashamed. I! Why was I ashamed? I had done nothing. I was innocent. I was worried about my baby. It was they who degraded themselves, who were worse than beasts, because animals do not torture each other, it was they who should have been ashamed. They should have the nightmares!"

I didn't care that I was shouting. Again my analyst was silent, then he reminded me that I was being moral and emotional, while our problem together

was one requiring a scientific approach; we must forget about moral judgments and be scientific, even
though, as he put it so delicately, morals might be
appropriate in other human relationships. I had
formed something of an emotional attachment to
him as is normal during analysis. That was the
speech that broke it. You can never remove morality
from your dealings with human beings; I told him
that is the beginning of Fascism.

As we settled ourselves in canvas deck chairs,
Emory sat in the captain's chair telling us that,
beyond the island, we would come to his favorite
part of the river, where great stone bluffs rise steeply
from the water on the east side. "Now they look like
bare rock," he says, "but you should see them in the
fall, sumac at the bottom, bright red, and woodbine
crawling up the rocks like flames."

He has nowhere to go but down, Aggie had said of
Emory; I looked at him in profile, and at his blond
hair and blue eyes and he looked like my cousin,
Hans, who used to go skiing at Garmisch. He went to
Israel and was killed there in 1948. Down, I thought,
how can they know the meaning of down? The
shame, the horror and the fear, we learned the meaning of down, I thought, we German Jews, and I looked
at Ginny and then Sol and I cried silently; let them
not learn it. Let them never know. It is enough, is it
not? But perhaps there is no vicarious sacrifice, no
martyrdom that serves for others, perhaps every
human being must ultimately sacrifice himself.

Now, with a sudden lurch, the motors started their noise and vibration, and the boat moved sluggishly backwards, away from the scene of the accident. We again moved inevitably toward what awaited us. We were going around the west side of an island, following the channel markers, further down the river. I had not said anything about turning back, I had not uttered my Cassandra "stop, stop now!" and I sat there, as I had sat on the train out of Berlin, unable to halt the flow of events, any more than I could stop the river from taking its inexorable course down to the sea. There was no turning back as there is never any turning back in the process of our lives. Ginny would struggle with her secret and her guilt; whatever business matter Frank and Emory had quarreled about, they would quarrel about again, or find a way to settle, Sol must accept the death of his wife, Aggie must follow where Frank led her, to labor union headquarters, to Navy installations, to picnics on sandbars with his wealthy partner, and she would go, complaining and questioning and without imagination.

And I? My son, Walter's son, who was conceived in Germany and born in Italy, my son was in graduate school now. I had let go of him. I had consciously and carefully let go of him, and he was independent. I believed that the only love in my life henceforth was that impersonal pity and compassion with which I treated my patients. I was wrong about many things, about my own capacity to love, about Aggie, for she would not follow, but lead this day. We cannot predict. Only I was right that sacrifices would be made, that I knew.

I heard Ginny say it was chilly and she thought she'd make some coffee; she went into the galley. My eyes fell on Frank; for what might he sacrifice himself? He looked neither like Ginny's romantic lover, nor a winner of wars, nor like a hero of the working classes. He was fat, his smile was broad, his cigar expensive, a contented capitalist, I thought.

Suddenly there was a scream. Frank leaped out of his chair, as though a spring unwound; he was through the door in one motion and I heard his voice boom out, "You're okay! You're all right, you're all right."

By the third phrase, the rest of us were on our feet. Emory had somehow slowed the boat, giving the steering wheel to Sol, and now Ginny and Frank appeared through the doorway.

"Thought you had a fire, didn't you, doll?" Frank had his arm around Ginny, and her face was white. She was shaking. "It's okay," Frank said to all of us, "a piece of paper caught fire, too near the top of the stove, it's all out. No danger at all."

Emory dove through the galley door and then appeared again. "Why did you scream so?" he said angrily to Ginny, who now was trying to smile. "You frightened us all!"

"She was scared," Frank said. "Woman's privilege, scream when you're scared. Isn't it, Gin?"

Ginny looked at him, as though suddenly realizing who he was, and backed away from his protecting arm. "Don't call me that!" she exclaimed angrily.

"No," Frank said bitterly, "I shouldn't call you that. It isn't your name."

"Here," Emory said to her, solicitous now, "sit down, Ginny, I'll get everybody a shot of scotch. I think we all need it."

When Emory had gone, Frank said to Ginny, "Have you ever met someone you haven't seen for years, like a teacher, or a high school football hero, and been disillusioned and found out they were just ordinary? And spoiled?"

"No," Ginny said, "I certainly haven't!"

When Emory came back and handed a glass to Frank, he said, "Thanks. I was too far from the door, and I couldn't leave the wheel."

Frank raised his glass, "Don't defend yourself. *L'chaim.* Luckily, it was nothing."

Ginny gulped hers down and then said, "I'm sorry I scared everybody."

Emory looked at her rather coldly. "You are touchy today, aren't you?" he said. Then he walked over to Sol. "Here, I'll take the wheel now," he said, brusquely.

"Fire is always frightening," Sol pontificated as he leaned against the railing.

Frank laughed, "You sound as though you've swallowed a PA system again." Under Sol's responding smile, I saw that his eyes were inward.

"Okay, Frank," Sol said, "When I see a fire," he touched his face, "I feel it. I got mine in a fire. Flying. The plane had already landed when it started burning.

I was being transported to a new duty station in the European theater, in Germany. I remember in the hospital I had a queasy feeling, I was the first rabbi to be sent as chaplain to that section of Germany immediately after V-E Day, and I was greeted with fire. Of course it was just a freak accident."

We were quiet, yet his description seemed to call for a response.

"Ahh, we're all on borrowed time," Frank said. "Did I ever tell you I was supposed to get mine at Okinawa?"

"No," said Sol, "what do you mean?"

"You were a chaplain for Army Air Force?" Frank asked. Sol nodded. "I was in Naval Air." Frank went on. "'Glad to have you gentlemen aboard,' they'd say, and then they'd notice I was a Jew. They tell me things have changed now. I wonder. . . . Well, I was a flight officer, but before they shipped me out to the Pacific I had some special signal corps training, they need an officer to go in with the signal corps ahead of the troops when they land on a beach somewheres, you're so loaded down with equipment you don't bother to carry arms, and the whole idea is to get the stuff installed so you can radio back what's happening."

Ginny shuddered audibly. "And my son wants to go in the Navy," she said.

"Peacetime Navy, that's nothing," Frank said. "Well, wc had a special little patch to show we'd been trained to put aerials in coconut trees without being seen by Japs, and off they sent me to General

Headquarters in Hawaii. So I waited around for orders. My God, there was nothing to do but wash my whites and salute officers for three weeks, and finally they sent me off on a flattop to assist the administrative officer. One time I was on leave in Honolulu and I met a fellow in the officer's mess wearing a patch like mine. I always thought it would save a lot of sparring around if civilians wore identification, too. Asked me my name, said I was the bastard whose orders got mixed up, I was supposed to relieve him while he went stateside, the typist got his serial number wrong, and meanwhile his captain changed his mind and told him he had to stay. Well, that was early you know, before we really got moving in the Pacific, and I knew the guy's ship and station and all that. They got theirs at Okinawa. To a man. Not one survived."

Sol was nodding his head. Emory at the wheel shrugged a little. "Yes, that's how it is," Frank went on; "a mistake in typing can be a man's fate, not even the whim of a Nazi or the venom of a Jap, just an error in a machine, when death is a game every man is playing. Yet, when you win, you feel guilt." Every weak, skinny, skeletal man or child who walked out of a concentration camp felt guilty for surviving, I thought, and I felt guilty for being naked. But what about those in America who just read the papers? Yes, what about the Allies who could have traded a few trucks for thousands of Jewish lives? And the British with their white papers? When you're alive, you're guilty, you've entered the conspiracy with the enemy. Can you ever atone for just living, when the rest of them are gone?

Suddenly Sol sounded angry, "Don't you realize you've only had a more dramatic experience of what happens to every human being? Don't you realize that the fundamentally religious person opens his eyes and sees the precariousness of human life and takes it in and believes anyway?" He shook his head. "During the war, that was synthetic religion, foxhole religion, I'm scared, I'll pray, no, I mean a deeper thing. Who can look upon the human condition and not acknowledge God? Who, without acknowledging God, can even open his eyes to the human condition?"

"Freud," I said automatically, "but he looked down on all religion. Look at the fantasies of history and mythology he had created in his later years. Freud could look at a single patient, yes, but at the human condition?" "Only with the help of God," Sol said. I wondered who was right, if there is a right.

Emory was uncomfortable with this kind of talk and he began to tell about his Army job, which was mostly basic training for infantry troops. It wasn't very heroic, but this, too, we don't choose, and the alphabetical order of one's name might determine as much as his heroism or lack of it. Emory taught marksmanship at Fort Bragg for forty-two months; Ginny had lived nearby after a while, and she hadn't minded the south too much. Aggie said promptly that she'd hated it; she'd had a civil service job in

Atlanta for a while, she said, and couldn't stand the way Negroes were treated. Sol and I, almost as if by agreement, left them there and went up to the roof of the cabin, where we sat in the sun, quite alone, the noise of the motor a little less penetrating up there.

"Frank," I said, "what sort of a man is this?"

"A mystery, like every human soul."

"Yes, rabbi," I mocked him a little.

"When his son was in my confirmation class, he began to show up at services." Sol said, "He even came to me."

"He came to you?"

The rabbi chuckled. "Women came to my grandfather, bless his soul, to see if their chickens were kosher, and men came with their old, torn prayer books. He should put them in the *genizah* or bury them with proper rites at least. What would he think of men and women who came to ask how to *daven*? How to *daven*, my grandfather wouldn't know how to answer. With him, Jews were born praying."

"Not anymore," I said.

"No, well, they come to me mostly for social services and psychiatry, because it says in the love-columns that you should go to your clergyman, but sometimes they come the way Frank did. I gave him Milton Steinberg to read and Rabbi Hertz's daily prayer book with the notes and explanations. He was groping, struggling. I can't violate a professional confidence, you know, something happened after the war, made him, he said, lose faith and pursue the almighty dollar consciously, he said, not unconsciously like the rest of them. He has a fine intellect, better than mine, I think."

"What makes you say that?"

"He knows what he's doing. One of us would have gone in there to Ginny, he did it sooner, he simply grasped the situation faster, didn't he?"

"A great deal more than intellect is involved in a response like his," I said, "fear, a flow of adrenalin, the male instinct to protect the female, something innate in the personality..."

"I'll tell you about the first time he came. He was furious. I don't remember what it was about any more, some social function planned for the confirmation class, but I remember what he said all right." Sol told me Frank had come into his office, his overcoat still on, and harangued him without even sitting down.

"'I thought the synagogue was different,' Frank had said, 'and the Temple. In my innocence, I thought people were different here, I don't have any pretensions of righteousness, God knows I don't come to services, but to find the same squabbles for power and importance, and the same women trying to run the social affairs that you find everywhere else. . . . Ahh, it's a shame! You PRAY, and then you go downstairs to an *oneg* and high hat one neighbor and try to speak to the Important People. I'm sick. The leadership, you preach at them about social conscience, and they don't vote and they don't even know any non-Jews.'

"I had stopped Frank, I had asked him why he wanted the Temple to be better than any other Jewish organization, or different. And then his mood changed, he'd sat down and pulled off his coat, and almost sobbed. 'Rabbi, I wanted to believe, all the time, that somewhere, somehow, there were people who were different, kind, warm, helpful, not competitive, not valuing the dollar more than anything else. Why aren't they here?'

"'Maybe they are,' I said; I named a few of the people who came week after week, some of them old and alone, and some of them truly devoted, quiet about it. He said he didn't know them, their kids weren't in the confirmation class. He said, how did they get that way? How did they have the discipline to come week after week, they weren't hired to do it like I was, he said. I was hurt and upset by the conversation, but I liked Frank, because he was trying to be honest. He said he didn't know how to pray, he said he used to think anybody who prayed was a hypocrite, but now he knew that wasn't right. Frank began to come to services, and then to a men's luncheon group that met together once a week and read the Bible. He had a daring kind of mind, he'd put together science and tradition and philosophy and ask frightening questions. Really. Will the Jewish community in America be able to survive affluence as the European community survived poverty? Is prayer self-hypnosis? He'd get very intense and then he'd laugh and shrug it off. What's wrong with

American society? He'd come back to that one often enough, he was searching for something, and I don't think he ever laid his hands on it. But I think he learned how to pray. He was looking for meaning and purpose; he liked Ecclesiastes best of all the books in the Bible, 'the most honest,' he said. 'You can have everything everybody is struggling for, money and home and family and prestige and still be miserable, and not know why. You can be pious and be miserable too, he used to say, so why do I go from one variety of misery to the other? It must be I like Jewish misery.'"

"Why did he say you brought him back to the fold?"

"I don't know. Frank and I have a strange friendship. He wants to have an authoritative word from me sometimes, other times he wants to negate my authority by familiarity, and, of course, a rabbi has no authority. All he can do is share what he knows of tradition and thought, and tradition is not binding on Reform Jews, it's a guide, not a yoke. Sometimes I thought Frank wanted a yoke. Sometimes I still think so."

I nodded to Sol. "But I still don't know what kind of person he is. What does he want?"

"Meaning," Sol said. "Meaning in his life, purpose, like all of us." What would psychiatry say everyone wanted? Tranquility, peace of mind—in a way, absence of neurosis or mental illness—but does that depend on finding meaning in life? I wondered.

❧ CHAPTER 10 ❧

*W*e were now approaching the locks and dam, a cement wall thrown across the river before us. There were guardhouses built on either side of this wall, and as Emory blew the horn of the boat, a tiny figure appeared from one of them. I didn't realize how high the wall was until I saw that doll-like human. Emory had slowed the boat almost to a standstill, the motor was quieter, we could feel the water rocking us ceaselessly. Emory's head appeared on a level with the roof where Sol and I had been talking, and he pointed out a rope near the front that Sol was to loop through a ladder after we entered the lock. "Leave plenty of slack," Emory warned, "the water will drop twenty feet." Sol knelt there, the rope in his hand, looking a little awkward.

"This is a new one on me," he said.

Earlier, Emory had told us all about the locks, as he kept telling us all about local matters, in his proprietary way. How they were used for flood control, navigation, and defense, how we must wait for a certain light to flash and the lock-master to signal before we would be admitted, how many tons of concrete were poured and millions of dollars spent in their construction. It amazes me how Americans are always claiming they have the biggest, and therefore in their eyes the best of everything. And it amazed me how Emory had memorized all these statistics.

But now we were drifting at the foot of the great gates, they were perhaps a hundred feet high and looked solid, not like gates at all, but like an impenetrable wall. We drifted broadside there in our boat, that now seemed so tiny, water below us, the wall before us, dwarfed.

The light flashed and, without any sound at all, a crack appeared in the huge wall as two sections began to swing open, the water boiling and choppy as the water within joined the free water of the river. The two sections opened only a little way, just enough to admit us, and Emory now started the boat very slowly, straightened it out, while he explained. Here we were entirely walled in by concrete, like a toy boat in a tremendous bathtub. Emory guided the boat to a place in the wall where a number of steel rungs were set in the cement. Sol now passed a loop of the rope through one of these rungs, and yelled to Emory that he'd done it. Again, the motor was silent.

Now the silence was frightening, as though a friendly and reassuring voice had stopped speaking in the middle of a sentence. Up on top of that immense barricade a uniformed man paced, the only motion anywhere in sight, and a cold knot grew in my stomach, I was walled in, impotent, and there was a man patrolling on a high, high wall, I felt I was in a camp with nothing to do but sit, wait, obey; I had gone on the train, and Walter had never completed his final mission of resistance, instead he had been captured and sent to Bergen-Belsen. He could never join me in Italy, or anywhere in this world, because September 1939 had come, and carried him along like a leaf on the river to his death, as I was carried to Maria's little hut. How unwillingly, unwittingly, we are committed to a course and a journey and a way. I knew I was holding myself rigidly, looking down at the canvas top of the boat, at my shoe and the threads of the canvas, coated with some waterproof material, some heavy paint, and I tried not to remember, I didn't want to remember. Then I noticed a strange sensation as the water began to leave the lock, to sink, it was not like falling, more like going down in an elevator, yet as I looked and saw the water falling away from the wall, leaving its wet mark there, I felt as though all the world were sinking, growing heavy, as though I were sinking into the canvas because there was a ball of heaviness growing inside me.

Sol had his back to me and I looked for something to focus my eyes on besides the walls and the man patrolling on top, and then I was relieved to see Ginny's red hair appearing, and her face as she climbed up the little ladder. First she went to see if Sol was managing the rope all right, and then she came and sat beside me.

"Did you know," she whispered, "that when Aggie and Frank built their new house, that she had herself quite a good time with the architect?"

I asked, "How did you know that?" I pulled my attention toward her like a fish way out on the end of a line. I focused on her wide, green eyes.

She smiled, mysteriously, "Oh, people saw them together, and I heard about it. He was from San Francisco, so he had to spend about a week here, and he came back much oftener than was necessary. Everybody said so."

"Do you mean they had some sort of an affair?"

Ginny looked surprised, "Why not? She's kind of an unhappy person, isn't she? I mean, after all, he was very attractive, and available."

You believe it because you would have done it, I thought to myself, and smiled at the old truth, how we always see our own faults in others! It was not Freud who said that but *Grossmutter*, yes, I thought, how other people are mirrors when we look at them, how we see ourselves there, instead of seeing them, how incapable we are of seeing something really other than ourselves.

"Perhaps you should just think of it as gossip," I told her, "so long as your husband and hers have to get along, at least while they have this business deal."

She pouted a little, "I'd rather they wouldn't get along," she said, then added, "You like Sol, don't you?"

"Hush," I answered.

She shook her head and whispered, "He isn't listening. I like him, too."

I tried to quiet her; her face was very close to mine, she was half-whispering, and I hoped he couldn't hear. "He and his wife seemed so happy together. I used to watch her at services looking up at him, adoring him, really, and once he kissed her after some holiday service, he was so protective and gentle, it looked so perfect, but now she's dead, and he'll have to raise those kids. How could God do that to him?"

How could God? The uniformed man still patrolled the wall, my stomach still held itself in a cold knot, but now at the far end of the lock, an opening appeared, a gate began to swing open, and Emory yelled up to Sol to release the rope, which he had played out as the water level sank below us. Now Emory started the motor, this time it was a reassuring sound, and Emory must have waved at the man in uniform, because suddenly he waved back. It was as though he broke a spell, the feeling of heaviness disappeared.

Now, as we moved forward toward the gate, my

stomach began to unfold, I breathed deeply, and I spoke a riddle to Ginny, "God or man?" I asked, and my mind raced over an old number, six million, and names: Walter, *Mutter*, *Vater*, and I could not answer my own riddle. "Israel," some said, but that, too, was part of the riddle, as was history, and my own unconscious, and even Ginny, looking for a human mirror so she could see herself in reverse, she virtuous, the other woman having an affair with a man. Would anyone on this boat be my mirror?

Ginny looked puzzled, "Let's go back on deck," she said, "the chairs are more comfortable than sprawling up here on the roof. Besides, I'm going to get sunburned if I stay here another minute." I followed her down the ladder, beckoning to Sol, who came, too.

The character of the river changed somewhat below the lock. It became wider and probably shallower, since it was dotted with low, marshy islands. The banks were not so steep nor the hills quite as high as they had been earlier in the day. The landscape seemed more pastoral, less dramatic, than before. Now a heron rose from one of the islands, the flapping of his wings as he mounted, sounding quite like a motor; Emory called our attention to a flock of ducks overhead, and said that this was one of the great natural waterways of the country, that wild birds had migrated along this river for centuries before the white man came, and would continue in spite of him. The low, marshy islands and shallow water were a great stopping place for these migrations, he told us, and many birds lived and bred here. How he loved this country!

Frank said rather abruptly, "I want to get back to our earlier discussion. There's one question I want to ask you, Emory: Why did you want to build a shopping center anyway? Falk's, as I understand it, is doing just fine."

"Of course it is," Emory's shoulders stiffened. "Here, Ginny, you take the wheel, will you?" Emory sat in a deck chair next to Frank. Emory's legs were muscular, his white shorts and T-shirt still white after his day in the country, his thick-soled shoes solid on the deck. He sat erect, yet easy, his arms resting on the wooden chair arms. Frank, next to him, slouched, looking more relaxed than he was.

"I'm glad you asked," Emory said, "but I'm not sure you can grasp the answer. This is a deliberate policy of mine: to do things not just to benefit the store, but to benefit the whole community."

"Hear, hear," said Frank dryly.

"Of course we're doing well at Falk's, but we have to protect our position as the finest department store in the Northwest. Not the biggest, the finest. Quality. This enclosed shopping center, the first in the country," Emory looked around at all of us, "Didn't you read about it last Sunday? This will be something absolutely unique. Local people will love coming there in the winter, out of the cold, and it will bring people from all over the country, for architectural and artistic interest. It'll be a real tourist attraction for our city. It's marvelous public relations, there'll be articles in magazines about it and the town and Falks will be known all over the country. Don't you agree?" he appealed.

"In other words," Frank growled, "you want prestige, and not profits."

"Prestige first and profits afterwards," said Emory, looking triumphant.

"Did it ever occur to you," said Frank, now sitting up and glaring at Emory, "that you'll lose your precious prestige just as fast as you lose your money?"

"We expect to absorb some losses the first few years," Emory said stiffly.

"If you don't get the big chain stores in there, Woolworth's, Montgomery Ward, or Sears, you won't pull in the people. And the only way you can make any money is to pull in the people, not tourists for once a year, but people who'll come back every week. And, if you don't give those big stores what they want, they'll go somewhere else, and you won't have Falk's Artistic Extravaganza, you'll have Falk's Folly! You'll lose your prestige and your shirt, too!"

"The trouble with you is you're completely lacking in imagination," Emory said coldly.

"You lack business experience!"

"Now that's a hell of a thing to say," Emory looked really angry, "I've been running Falk's for almost twenty years."

"Yeah, just the way Daddy handed it to you,"

Frank said, and I saw Emory clenching his fists. "Besides, I didn't go in with you to absorb losses. I made that clear from the beginning. I want this to be a profitable operation."

Ginny turned her head away from the wheel, "Why don't you buy him out, Emory? Why do you keep on trying to deal with him?"

"Listen, Gin," Frank said, getting to his feet and puffing his cigar to relight it. "He can't afford to buy me out, and he knows it."

Emory was on his feet, too, and his arm had gone back as though he was going to swing at Frank. Sol stood between the two men. Aggie's remark, "He has nowhere to go but down," flashed through my mind.

"Wait," Sol said, "sit down, gentlemen, sit down."

"Why should we?" Emory growled, but they sat again, glaring at each other, shifting in their chairs.

Emory said, "Virginia!" very sharply. "Please keep out of this discussion."

"He wants to ruin you!" she screamed hysterically. "He . . ." I stopped her by moving next to her and putting my hands on her shoulders. "It isn't related to their problems at all," I said softly. She looked at me, I patted her shoulders, and she closed her mouth, and turned back to her piloting. Then she threw one more remark at her husband, "But you can afford to buy him out, can't you?"

"I think I could," Emory said, "we have a buy-sell agreement with a stated amount for buying each other out. My attorneys drew it up largely as a protection for me because he's considered such a shrewd operator."

"Great guys, your attorneys," Frank jeered. "You know what, Aggie? He's even got an insurance policy on my life. If I died, he'd get more than you right now, and you'd get a lot. That's where he did a smart thing, it isn't the option I had on the land that's valuable to him, it's my cleverness in business. He needs me, by God, he does!"

"Frank," Emory said loudly, extending his hand, "I don't like to talk business on a holiday. Let's suspend it till Wednesday morning in my office, about 11, huh?"

Frank took his hand momentarily. "I thought that was the whole point of this trip, to talk things over, and nothing's settled, is it? You haven't even listened to me once!"

"Well, maybe you wanted to talk when you finagled this trip, but I . . ."

"Finagled! Hell, you were the one who insisted," Frank said. "Privacy and leisure and all that, and then when you brought Sol, I thought you were scared and wanted somebody to keep the peace."

"That's rich!" said Emory. "I thought out here, with the beauties of nature, maybe I could get through your thick head that I want to build something beautiful."

"Is that any reason I can't give Woolworth's the southeast corner? They've looked at the plans and made a traffic study and they insist, and without them, we're dead."

"That's every reason!" Emory shouted again. "The architect planned it that way. You can't go telling a man like Neumann to change things around to suit a dime store!"

"It's my land," Frank said wearily.

"Your option," Emory corrected him.

"My option," Frank said, "but it's a lot more than my option now. I've been spending almost full time trying to get tenants, and you've been spending almost full time frustrating me. If a tenant wants something, a good tenant, it's good business to give it to him, isn't it?"

"No!" Emory shouted. "Why can't you see my point? This is more than a shopping center, it's an architectural monument!"

"To a stupid idea."

"Some people just have no feeling for beauty," Emory said.

Aggie spoke: "Frank does, if you'd seen our new house, you'd know it. He picked a young architect who'd won a prize."

Ginny interrupted, "And he was quite a prize, wasn't he?" I patted her shoulder again, "No," I whispered to her, "no."

"Wednesday morning, Emory," Frank said wearily, "God willing, if your attorneys can figure out a way to pay me what it's all worth."

"Are we going to turn back soon?" Sol asked.

"Why, it's only 5:30," Emory said. "It won't be dark till 9 and we'll have plenty of time to go for dinner after we get back. There's a beautiful spot down the river I want you to see, then we'll head back. I know you and Charlotte appreciate lovely things, at least I want you two to have a good day! How about some ginger ale? Or a martini?" Emory got to his feet, "Come and help me, Lotte, while Ginny pilots."

I followed him into the little galley and he turned to me. "I'm baffled," he said. "A man like Frank baffles me. I suppose he hates me because of my position. It must give him some sort of pleasure to humiliate me. Of course, Ginny doesn't like him at all. She doesn't say so, but I suppose he tried to make advances to her. Some men do. She's a damned attractive woman, isn't she?" I nodded, standing there watching him preparing the drinks, stirring in ice, shaking, pouring, just so. "What motivates a man like that?" he asked me.

I shook my head, "I don't know," I said. "You see, you can't say 'a man like that'—like what? I can't put him in any category. Categories don't help us understand people."

"No, of course," Emory said, "but I am going to try to buy him out, and he's right, it will be very hard for me to raise the money in one lump sum, and that was a condition of the agreement. I made it that way so he couldn't buy me out. Huh," he snorted. "And my business is not what it was a year ago when we started this project. It won't be easy. But I can't work with him any more. I've never had a partner, and I don't want one now." The drinks were on the tray.

"Here we go! You first," and I went before him up the ladder into the sunshine.

We were crossing a wide place in the river, without islands. "Now we are really at Lake Pepin," Emory lectured, "this is a wide, deep lake formed by the confluence of the Chippewa and Mississippi Rivers. The Chippewa is fast and brings in rocks and sand that hold back the water, a natural damn. There was a terrible accident here in 1864, a steamship, side-wheeler, capsized during a storm. Forty-two people drowned."

"Really, you told us about that already. You are cheerful," Aggie said.

"But, it's so different today," he said, "that's one reason I like to tell my guests, first the buoys in the water," he pointed to a red one bobbing near us. "And also the markers on the shore." I saw a huge white X painted on a tree. "Besides that," Emory added, "I doubt if you know it but, when we left the marina, I told the attendant when to expect us. If we don't show up, he calls the Coast Guard. Routine. They love to practice rescue operations, gives them a chance to play with their helicopters."

"No thanks," I thought.

We had come to the end of the lake. "See here," Emory took the wheel from Ginny and steered toward a large rock that rose abruptly from the water. "This is what I wanted you to see. Isn't it dramatic? And now we turn back." Emory cut through the water so the boat tipped to one side, and I felt insecure, knowing that only a few pieces of wood lay between the cold river and me. The wind had come up and the sky clouded over, and the sound and vibrations of the motor increased as we pushed upstream against the current. Would we ever get home?

❧ Chapter 11 ❧

*T*he sky was dark with clouds now, the wind blew alternately warm and chill, and we knew a storm was coming.

Frank and Sol climbed up to pull a canvas roof arrangement over the deck where we were sitting, to keep the rain off. Emory was piloting again. I was fatigued from the constant noise and vibration of the motor. We rode the broad river in a thin shell of wood, a frail thing, driven by controlled explosions of gasoline, in a motor I dimly understood, along shores that were unfamiliar to me, how we trust in our brain power, not our own, but of others, the boat-builders, the motor-makers, how we ride along, not understanding the forces that propel us, it's all right, isn't it, as long as we can steer? But can we? And I thought of Freud, and his genius, and his greatness, who recognized the great submerged bulk of the unconscious, and asked, who is steering this ship? Who recognized the half-human creatures in steerage and the sub-human creatures in the engine room, and all the dark passages leading them to the bridge and the captain's room, yet without them, how could the captain function? Papa Freud.

Emory seemed to enjoy a certain exaltation as the storm approached, he was going to show us all he knew about navigating, he was going to be the natural leader who brought us through this challenge. His spirits rose, and he began to joke with the others, as he had not done on the whole journey. Sol seemed a little more alert, but mostly unchanged. He sat up a little straighter, talking to Ginny about the Temple, and I watched her lying in the chair, kitten-like, stretching a little in the middle, then putting her hand behind her head so that her breast was outlined for him to see, and I saw his eyelids droop just a little, as he noticed her.

"Do you know what I'm going to do if you buy me out?" Frank sang out to Emory.

"Maybe I won't," said Emory.

"I've got a plan," Frank leaned forward in his chair, his elbows on his knees. He looked up with a sparkle in his eye. I felt the youthfulness and the eagerness that must have attracted Ginny first, and then Aggie. "We're going to Israel," Frank had to raise his voice because the rain and motor were noisy, and it rang out like a challenge.

"Tour?" said Ginny.

"Maybe a lot more than a tour. I'm going to look for a way to invest my money there. It's a dream I've had for a long time, and we'll stay a while, too, get the feel of the land. And go away and then come back again."

"You're crazy," Emory's voice was also a little raised. "You can get much better returns right here."

Frank turned to Sol and he was laughing. "Now, who doesn't understand the higher things in life?" Then he spoke to Emory, "You be an esthete, Emory, I'll be an idealist."

Aggie said, "Oh, Frank, I'd love to go" and there was a sudden smile on her face, perhaps the first that day. She moved over to Frank and suddenly bent down and kissed him. He looked up, surprised and pleased.

"What do you want to go there for?" Emory asked again, "A little dinky country, dry, hot, apt to be blown off the map any minute, when you've got all this?" His gesture was big, and if we could have seen the river and the hills, it would have been expressive. But the canvas covering cut off our view.

"You tell him, Sol," Frank said. "Tell him what you told me that day."

"You mean that there is a vocation for the Jewish people?" Frank nodded. Sol went on. "Some Jews feel it and some don't. But it's there. A demand. A call. A divine mandate."

"Well, I believe that," Emory said, "In the sense that the highest moral conduct is demanded of us. And I try to live up to it."

"Moral conduct?" Frank spoke, "Yes! And martyrdom! Also yes. And sacrifice? Again, yes."

Ginny shuddered, "You talk like the middle ages and the ghetto and all that. It's paranoid, isn't it?" she looked at me.

"Do you think so, Lotte?" Frank said.

I shook my head. I saw Sol's face gathering the shadows to itself, the eyes deep, the mouth a dark line, and the scar black and solid, and he said, "The idea of sacrifice can never be alien to the Jewish people." I didn't want to listen to anything about sacrifice. Was Walter's death a sacrifice? . . . No, I couldn't accept that. I couldn't call the six million deaths a sacrifice . . . to what? To whom?

"I don't know what you mean," Ginny said.

Sol shook his head and said gently, "Would you know what I mean by holiness? *Kadosh*, and he began to try to explain to her. "*Kadosh* means holy, *kiddush* means hallow, or sanctify, make holy, *kiddush hashem*, you know what that means?" Ginny shook her head. "To make the name holy, the name of God, and how do we do that?"

Ginny sighed, "Obeying the commandments, I suppose."

Sol said, "Yes, but in Jewish history, *kiddush hashem* came to mean martyrdom, because often the choice was desecration of the name of God, or death." I didn't want to listen to this old rationalization.

Ginny shivered, and Frank said, "Concern for one's fellow-man, justice, isn't that the most important?"

"And love," said Sol.

"Even without love," Frank said.

Jews look at themselves in the mirror of humanity, they trace their history, they celebrate their deliverance from slavery in Egypt. They can only see themselves in that very humanity which causes them suffering. And I, on this boat, am like my people floating with other people down the treacherous river of time. I have suffered my own sufferings, and I have endured the sorrows of others, and received the confessions of some, and the guilt of some, and shared the hurts of some, and without them, I am nothing. I am incomplete, unfinished; there cannot be a psychiatrist without a patient, a mother without a child, nor a human being without another human being. Could there have been Jews without Egypt? Without Persia and Rome and Spain and Poland and Germany? Without Israel? Ah, God of Israel, what is our vocation?

"I'm going to Israel," Frank said, "because I'm searching for something that I've never found, and if it's anywhere on earth, it's there, somewhere, in the heart of the Jewish people. But, remember one thing, Ginny, sacrifice is real. It is a fact of Jewish life, now and always. Maybe it's a fact of all life."

Without them, I was thinking, I would be nothing. Does it matter if God is in space or my unconscious? In heaven or in my heart (perish the unscientific symbol)? He is there. I am a Jew and stuck with Him, and His Moses, and His commandments. I am a Jew and blessed, because, though each of us is incomplete and imperfect and guilty and scarred, we have community, as Sol had said. Nothing in the whole universe has the unity of God. Everything else is confused and torn and eternally divisible, into the cell, the atom, the electron, the neutron, the neuroses, the shattered psyches.

I remembered Rilke's lines, "*Du, Nachbar Gott.*" He imagined God as a neighbor in the adjoining apartment. I thought, the Jews speak to each other about God, but they do not address him as Rilke did, as though just on the other side of a wall. The wall is not a thin wall between apartments but it is like the wall of the lock, concrete and impenetrable, we have lost the signal to open it. Yet we are commanded to love Him; perhaps Rilke, like me, has lost his language, for he had a Jewish parent and a German upbringing. I know no German word for *Rachmonot*, the tenderness and mercy of God, or as some translations have it, loving kindness. Is there a Hebrew word for "*angst?*" (Anxiety is a weak English translation) Or *shrechlichkeit* (a condition of terror or horror)? Are there English words for "*Torah*" (the first five books of the Bible, the teaching, the wisdom, the tree of life) or *Mitsva* (doing a good deed which is also a commandment) or *Gestalt*? How could I find the language to speak to Him, to open the barrier to God?

I remembered a pious man who said, "God turned his back on us, the German Jews, but first we turned our backs on Him." We lost our language, we broke the mirrors of Jewish history, and then it was as though history turned on us and broke the mirrors of love, ourselves seen in the eyes of those who loved us, for history caused them to perish. Still, we had to live in the modern world offered to us by the Enlightenment, even by the Austrians and Germans who liberated us from the ghettoes, and cancelled many of the laws that restricted our lives, although they didn't cancel their anti-Semitism.

I must look in the eyes of those around me here: of Sol, of Frank, I could pray for vision, I thought, and I despaired of the human vocabulary, for vision surely means seeing, but also more than seeing, insight, foresight, understanding, prediction, wisdom, and also love, and everything we pray for God has already given us, if we but knew.

The voices around me had stopped. There was a great rumble of thunder and only a few seconds later a flash of lightning that showed brightly through our canvas top. A rush of cold air came at us, and I shivered. Suddenly, everyone was talking at once. Sol had seen that I was cold and draped his jacket around my shoulders. Ginny announced she was going to get more coffee and Emory said we should all sing and began "happy is the day when the army gets its pay." Everyone joined him in the conspiracy not to notice the storm.

❧ CHAPTER 12 ❧

*T*he rain pelted the top of the canvas like bullets, the motor, moving us upstream against the current, and the choppy waves raised by the wind, was even noisier now, and I felt the explosions of each cylinder like a pulse, strong, but too rapid, the pulse of a strong man running, the pulse of the mechanical beast that we all depended on for our safety. How we depend on each other, I thought, on unknown persons, on those who built this boat and designed it, and made the parts for it, on those who marked the channel in the river, and built the locks. The lock? How could we possibly get through the lock in the storm? I stood up and looked through the window where Emory was looking. I could see nothing but black water, choppy waves, gray sky and rain everywhere, slanting down, blocking out the view. The hills were blotted out, as though they had never been. The river seemed boundless as the ocean, but then I saw a buoy bobbing on our left.

Emory spoke between his gritted teeth, "One more, I'm right on channel."

As the boat pitched and rocked, Sol's jacket swung awkwardly and heavily from my shoulders and I went back and sat beside him. Sol moved his deck chair closer to mine. Aggie was sitting beside Frank, her hand tucked between his arm and the side of his chest in an odd, childish gesture of affection. He patted her fingertips absently while he looked out at the little patch of water and rain visible from the small opening in the canvas at the back of the boat.

Sol spoke to me quietly. "I'm a little ashamed of my outburst to you this afternoon," he said.

"But why?" I asked.

"All that talk about community. I was wrong to look backwards to my grandfather's day, as though it was some sort of golden age, it wasn't. The community I talked about, that will only be at the end of days. Here we are, in the storm, on a small boat, there is something so primeval about this, the waters above and the waters below, life is full of danger and terror always."

"Do you really think we are in danger?" I asked.

Sol shrugged his shoulders. "I don't really know. This is a good boat, and Emory knows what he's doing, and there's the Coast Guard." There was another rumble of thunder followed very quickly by lightning that lit up his face and the smile that mocked his scar. "I didn't know I was in danger that day in the war" he touched his cheek where the scar lay. "We are so ignorant, so dependent, our life is so complex." His voice tapered off a little. "You know the Sabbath is supposed to be a foretaste of the world to come, the peace of the Sabbath is like one-sixtieth of the peace of the world to come."

"Yes, I know," I said.

Sol said with some irony, "Emory has had Sabbath on Monday, on the river. Well, I meant, I've had a foretaste of that community I spoke of, too, with my wife, with Frank, today with you. It's good to talk with you."

"Frank?" I asked.

"You see, after we became friends, I watched him. The good he does, he does very quietly. He sent a couple of students to Israel last year, he's supporting a young man studying for the rabbinate, and another boy studying social work at the U. He talks about profits in a loud voice, and he dishes his money out quietly."

"That kind of charity, individual favors, that isn't always the best," I said.

"It isn't like that. They don't know who's helping them. He's a sensitive man, and gentle."

"If you say so," I said, wondering.

There was another roll of thunder, and this time a longer interval before the lightning flashed.

"You see," said Sol, "the storm is probably blowing over. We may not be in danger at all."

"Perhaps not," I said, though the wind and the waves and the jolting and bobbing of the boat seemed to be shaking my spine unmercifully, if only this giant claw that held me would let me down, would release me for a moment.

"Most people pray when they're in trouble," Sol said, "but I turn away when trouble comes. Yet, I need God then, too. It's easier for me to give thanks than to beg for help." Sol covered his face with his hands for a minute. "He holds us all in His hand," he said, and rose from the chair and, turning his back to all of us, stood, his long legs braced, one hand on the railing, looking out at the water and the rain. He rocked his body a little, not with the rhythm of the motor, but in a far more ancient and familiar manner. Then Frank was on his feet, standing beside Sol, wordlessly, facing out into the storm. He, too, rocked himself; they were praying.

How terribly hard it is for us to pray in this generation, for who has found the language that will speak for us, who has found words for our lips that can speak for the whole human being? We split ourselves into mind and body, and we cannot put ourselves together again and speak from the depths, I will lift mine eyes to the mountains from whence cometh my help, that was my need, for help, but the mountains were blotted out by the rain, no Temple stood on those barren hills of the new world, and the help of God is not a hand reaching out to still the waters, it is far deeper and more subtle than that, I wait for a new teaching and a new way to God, Who is both transcendent and within, but I have no language for prayer. I cannot summon myself to this task, I am too incomplete, too divided.

After a while, Sol sat beside me again, not speaking, but with his hands at his sides, not seeking to cover his face or his eyes, as they had, somehow, all day. He looked more alert, more alive, less sleepy.

The boat began to move slowly, as though it were climbing up a hill. Emory said, "I'm going to have to put more gas in the tank," and then the motor stopped. I felt fear climbing into my stomach. The noise of the motor stopped, at first it seemed terribly quiet, and then, as the boat began to lurch and slip sideways into the trough of the waves, I heard the water slapping the boat, the rain falling on the roof, the wind hurtling down the valley, the canvas flapping, and, far off, the rumble of thunder. It became darker, and I could see no lights anywhere, no other boats, no farmhouses, though my view was small, cut off by the cabin, and by the canvas. Rain began to hit my arm and I moved my chair toward the center. Emory said, "Let's not get the boat off balance." He came up from the cabin, lugging a red can of gasoline, swearing a little as the door swung at him and almost knocked him back down the stairs. Frank jumped up to hold the door, and Emory directed him to open the tank, and he poured in the gasoline.

Emory then said, "I don't want to frighten anybody, but there are life jackets under the bunks, and well, that's where they are, if anybody's not a good swimmer."

Sol said, "I'll get them," and backed into the door of the cabin. He returned with an armload of the awkward life jackets and I saw that he had an orange one buckled on. He distributed one to each of us. I put mine on, but the others did not. I put it on not because I believed intellectually in the danger, but because I was beginning to feel it, and fear had better be dealt with lest it paralyze one.

Frank and Aggie had their life belts lying across their laps. "I don't think it's a clear and present danger, Falk," Frank said lightly, placing his trust in Emory, not for his money, but for his very life.

Emory had the motor going again, and that was a comforting sound, but suddenly the wind came up. The canvas was flapping and began to tear in one corner. Ginny said she'd go into the cabin, except she was sure she'd be sick, and we all sat right where we were. The waves were high, much higher than I dreamed they could get on a river. They began to slap up on the deck, and cold spray and rain and damp were everywhere. Emory had a hard time getting the boat out of the trough of the waves, and when he did, we no longer rode smoothly. It was rise, rise, then the bow of the boat would suddenly dip and the water would come running over the deck, and off, and rise, rise, dip, slap, a hard bump, like hitting a rock while driving on a gravel road, rise, dip, rise, dip, bump. It was uncomfortable, but not unbearable, and one began to wonder how the boat was made, like an eggshell, or like a battleship? What would happen if the ribs began to split from this pounding, or the canvas gave way and water began to come in from underneath? The waters above, the waters below, the waters imprisoned in the locks and the waters of freedom. I suddenly thought it might have been better if we had reached the lock by now.

It was quite dark except for sudden flashes of lightning, when one would see nothing but a wild landscape of water, and the rocks on the opposite shore might seem quite close because the light was so bright. My ankles were wet and cold, my cotton shirt was sticking to my back because of the wet, and my shoes were soaked. Nobody tried singing or jokes any more. I wondered how long it would be. A flash of lightning showed an island, where no island should be. It looked no more than 10 feet from the side of the boat.

Only Emory could see what lay ahead. "God damn!" he screamed, when he saw it, almost sobbing, "I must have missed the buoy!" He swung the boat around violently, my chair tipped and I slipped on the wet deck and Sol's hand firmly gripped my arm and set me back in place. Now I stood up, hanging onto the doorframe of the cabin, looking through the window at the water ahead, but the boat's running lights showed very little, Emory was guessing at the channel. Another flash of lightning showed water, only black and turbulent water ahead, no buoy, but I thought water was better than islands or rocks, and now the wind howled even louder than the motor.

Suddenly there was a terrible shudder through the boat. I heard a scream, I saw flashes of light, I heard a terrible sound of breaking wood, and I was thrown into cold, black water, deep, choking, swallowing it, brain numb, body fighting upward for air, clumsy with shoes and life jacket, and then my head came up, I caught a breath, a wave splashed and broke over my head, nearly choking me again, and I tried to use my arms to keep myself up. I could see nothing, no boat, no people. I heard water and wind, and a strange howling noise, a horn, a horn? Pushed up to the crest of another wave, I saw red and green lights blinking off to my right. What could that be? Another wave splashed over me and again I saw the lights. Perhaps it was the Coast Guard boat, I thought, will I ever stay afloat till they find me? I was shivering, my teeth were chattering, I thought I should get my shoes off, but couldn't imagine how I could reach my feet with the life jacket under my arms, and with waves almost drowning me. I tried to float in the life jacket, but I was tossed and thrown, another crest, another flash of lightning, and I saw our boat, lying on one side, the front end broken off, simply gone, and the motor crazily high in the air. I tried to shout, but water filled my mouth. I turned myself around, to go toward the wreckage. The others might have held onto their life jackets. The Coast Guard boat was coming closer now, throwing out a search light, its fog-horn bawling, its red and green lights blinking, and I thought, hurry! Hurry!

The next time the lightning flashed, I saw someone clinging to the boat, perhaps two people, and I began to try to swim toward it, though without the lightning, I would lose my sense of direction every time as the waves tossed me up and over, and I thought I would be in cold, stormy water forever, my chest hurt, water kept filling my mouth, I gasped for air, and I thought forever would soon be over, I was drowning, it was the end of my days, and I struggled toward the wreckage, thunder rumbling, fog-horn blowing, lights flashing.

It was then that I became a witness. Lightning ripped open the sky, and lasted, not for a second, but it must have been for twenty seconds. I saw layers of thick, gray clouds in the sky, the rain streaking down, and then I saw someone struggling in the water.

"Help!" she shrieked and one arm shot up, bare, "help." I saw black hair and knew it must be Aggie. She was near the wreck, and Frank was clinging to the side of it, and I saw him jump away and start to swim toward her as Emory yelled, "Don't! You can't make it!" But I saw Frank swimming toward her powerfully, the light from the sky brighter than day, crueler than the sun, and he reached out to her and she clutched at him, and then darkness, horrible darkness, complete darkness, like a black curtain, but then the Coast Guard ship came, hooting and crooning, throwing its yellow search lights, and the lights crossing the water, sweeping across the water where they had been, and God! Dear God, it was empty. No heads, no swimmers, nothing but wild waters. They picked me up then, and Sol and Ginny and Emory, who were clinging to the wreck. Ginny wept, and Sol wept, and Emory was white and silent and frightened.

❖ CHAPTER 13 ❖

*W*hen I walked from my apartment to the Temple, past well-kept lawns, under the shade of the big elms so carefully planted in straight lines along the street, I walked slowly. Sol had begged me to come to his office that morning; the funeral was going to take place in the afternoon. Wasn't this reality, the neat lawns, the sun shining on the cars that moved past me, the cars stopping at the red light on the corner? How could I believe that Frank and Aggie were dead, drowned in a storm?

I carried a book. I had tried to think of what I would say to Sol, and I had found part of a poem by C. Day Lewis that I wanted to read to him. It is called, "The Great Magicians":

But the hollow in the breast
Where a god should be,
That is the fault they may not
Absolve nor remedy.

I believed that all of us on the boat that day had that fault, that hollow, except, possibly, Frank. No magicians could remedy it except the magician in our deepest selves. I began to think about Frank. I remember the way Frank spoke about Israel, and the moment when he moved along the side of the boat to Sol and they prayed. I wanted to tell Sol about my grandmother and the mirror, and say that Frank had many human souls for mirrors. Now, after his death, the image may right itself, no longer reversed, but true. These were the things I planned to try to say to Sol, even though, as I walked along, I didn't believe it was really necessary. Somehow, Emory ought to be coming to my door, and I would say I couldn't come, so the trip would be cancelled. Or, perhaps if we went, we would turn back after our picnic on the sandbar, or just before we entered the locks, or, if Emory had seen that one buoy... but we didn't, and he hadn't.

I pulled open the heavy, wooden door of the Temple, entered the cool hall, and rather than facing the office girl, I tapped directly on Sol's door. His office is small, carpeted, and lined with books. He beckoned me to a chair and sat down behind his desk. His face looked deeply lined, troubled, his eyes burned like candles with black flames, and the scar seemed bigger, more contorting than ever.

"Before we talk about today, about this afternoon, there is something else I must say to you," he began.

I nodded, setting the book in my lap and waiting, observant, patient.

"When we went walking in the woods, I shouldn't have spoken to you as I did. I twisted everything. I said things that weren't true at all. Of course I took a lot of time away from my wife and family, but I don't resent it. I had to do it. I have to believe in what I did and in what I'm doing, or I wouldn't be myself at all. At least I have to try to believe. My wife loved me, I know that, and she loved what I was, what I must be, wouldn't she, then, love what I've become?"

"Yes," I said, "you're telling me that being a rabbi is part of you. That you couldn't change, or do half a job. Is that it?"

"That's it, yes, that's it. Not only the activities in the community, but the seeking, the searching."

"I wish to tell you something," I found myself saying, "something I seldom tell anyone. You know that many psychiatrists and psychologists, people in professions like mine, choose this work not because they are emotionally strong, but precisely because they need help themselves, because they hope that by helping others they may gain insights into themselves. Many do and I include myself. I have been thinking about you, Sol, and wondering why you became a rabbi. Was it perhaps not because you had faith and belief, but because you were seeking them? Because you wanted faith, because it was so important to you? And I want to tell you something else, too, Sol, I had many traumatic experiences when I lost my husband. I suppose if I could recover, I could love another man. I keep trying. And you, too, Sol, you may never attain perfect faith, but is that a reason to stop trying?"

He came from behind his desk and he held my face between his two hands, I felt the warmth of his hands on my cheeks, and he kissed my forehead. Standing there he said, "You will love again. I have faith in that if in very little else. And you're right about me, I never thought about myself in those terms, but of course you're right."

Now he sat down in a chair next to mine, "I can't thank you enough, Charlotte."

"Wait." I opened my book and read him the poem about "the hollow in the breast where a god should be."

"Long ago" I told him, "I read this in an English class and it has stayed with me. The great magicians, I think, are alchemists, scientists with new inventions, doctors with new cures, maybe political leaders, all without a remedy for our hollow souls. What do we need? A god, or one God, or love?

"I see," said Sol, "you think Frank might have had love or God in his soul." I nodded.

Sol continued, "Do you remember the flash of lightning and the sound of the boat horn? Could you see what happened?"

"Partly."

"I was right beside Frank when the lightning flashed. It lasted a long time. It was eerie how green it was and how distinctly you could see everything. And that horn blowing. Before that, I had the wild feeling I was at Mount Sinai on Judgment Day with green fire and thunder rumbling, and those horns like the *shofar*. I saw Aggie out there at the same instant, that thin arm in the black water, and heard her cry. Frank looked at me for an instant and then: that's how I know. It was as though he said, "Goodbye, I must try this even if I don't make it. I must.""

"Because he loved her?"

"Because he was Frank, because he had to be who he was, a man who takes action like when Ginny started the fire. It was his personality, if you will. He couldn't have lived afterwards if he had stood by while she drowned. It was his whole self, his whole faith, to do what he did. To dare, to do. It was thinking about him that made me see I can't be different either."

"He might have thought of his children."

"They're not babies. Robert's in graduate school, and the girl is in college. And, if he thought about it, he also knew Emory, he knew Emory would be honorable enough to make decent financial arrangements for the kids, and he's done it already. Turned over all that life insurance money to a trust fund for them."

"But Frank couldn't have thought of all that in one moment."

"No, but also, yes. It might have been part instinct. He knew what had to be done, he was called, and he answered."

It was then that I felt I must write everything that had happened. I told Sol I was going to write this story because the only language of prayer that we now can understand is the language of action. Because there are people in this world like Frank, who have whatever faith they need to perform the necessary action.

A few hours later, I sat in the sanctuary, near the back. The Temple was crowded with people; it was hot and the sun was streaming through the great dome, one ray hitting the gold letters of the Ten Commandments above the ark. I wanted Frank and Aggie to be alive, but two coffins, covered with flowers, were placed below the reading desk and I must believe they were there, their bodies, if not the uncontainable memories we have of them; their corpses were truly in those coffins.

The cantor sang the most lonely, sad chant in all the liturgy, *El Mole Rachamim* (God, full of compassion.) I had heard it before and I would hear it again, and the tears rose in my eyes and my throat began to hurt. Sol spoke about Frank and about Jacob, who wrestled beside the dark waters, and I thought: what if Freud had read the Bible instead of the Greeks? The heroes are long gone, long dead, more dead than my friends, but all about us, men and women are wrestling in the darkness. Some succumb, and others emerge, as

Frank did, and as Sol will do, whole but scarred.

They recited the Kaddish and the funeral ended, except that there is never an end to any human lives while others can ponder and remember them. And Sol and I remember.

About the Author

This is Ruth Firestone Brin's first novel after publishing twelve other books. She published poetry and articles in many periodicals, and reviewed books for several years for *The Minneapolis Star Tribune* and currently *The American Jewish World*. She taught at Macalester College and the University of Minnesota. She is well known in the Jewish community because her liturgical work appears in the current prayerbooks of the Conservative, Reconstructionist and Reform movements.